It has been seventeen years since the event that killed most of the people on the planet. The violence that swept the country for so long is gone, and Ben and Lila are now living a peaceful existence in their Yellowstone community. But more trouble is looming, and when their daughter Katie, now sixteen and going by the name of Cat, and eleven other teenagers leave to explore the country, that trouble hits home.

When two of the teens, one near death and the other deep in shock, return to Yellowstone a month later with the story that one member of the group is dead and the rest have scattered after a vicious attack by a new enemy, Ben and Lila know they must go after their daughter and her friends. But where? And are they way too late?

Taking up from the events of **Eden Lost** and moving ahead eight years, **Eden's Legacy** shifts between the adventures of Ben and Lila and those of their daughter Cat, a "different" girl who relates more easily to animals than she does to humans.

The final chapter in the *Eden Rising Trilogy*, **Eden's Legacy** has Ben and Lila meeting old friends, discovering what has happened across the rest of the globe, and asking the question: will their new world ever know peace?

EDEN'S LEGACY

Andrew Cunningham

ISBN-13: 978-1530437023
ISBN-10: 1530437024

Books by Andrew Cunningham

Wisdom Spring
All Lies
Deadly Shore
Eden Rising
Eden Lost
Eden's Legacy

Children's Mysteries
(as A.R. Cunningham)

The Mysterious Stranger
The Ghost Car
The Creeping Sludge
The Sky Prisoner
The Ride of Doom

ACKNOWLEDGMENTS

I would like to thank my copyeditor/proofreader/wordsmith extraordinaire, Marcia Kwiecinski, for the outstanding job she's done on my last two books. She is proof of the value of having your finished product picked apart by a professional.

And as always, none of my books would happen if I didn't have the total love, support, and enthusiasm of my wife, Charlotte. It means everything to me. Thank you!

To Mom,
With Love

Prologue

We called it the great migration.

It was a joke, of course, always said with a wink and a smile. A knowing understanding among parents. In truth, it was the only way we could deal with our fear. Our lives were about to change forever and we all knew it. We also knew that there was absolutely nothing we could do about it.

We had been in Yellowstone for eight years—eight of the happiest years we could imagine. The six years we had spent on the shores of Fontana Lake back east had, despite challenges, been a peaceful and maturing time for us amongst the stillness of the forest. But we never realized how lonely we had been. The fire that drove us out was really a blessing. Although the trip to Yellowstone was long and rife with danger—was there any trip in this new world that wasn't long and dangerous?—the result was worth it.

In Yellowstone, living around other people (but not too close) gave us a sense of community. We made close friends, while also deepening our connection with nature. Discovering that my brother—assumed lost in the event of so many years ago—was still alive filled me with tremendous joy, and over the years a deeper bond had formed than what we had known as children. Our parents would have been overjoyed that we both survived and had found each other.

For Katie, the move to Yellowstone meant so much more than even we could have envisioned. Our life story was as much about her as it was about Lila and me. Now sixteen—the age Lila was when the world turned upside down—Katie had a fire raging inside her. Her thirst for discovery far eclipsed anything that Lila and I ever felt.

With her shiny raven hair flowing over her shoulders, and looking like a carbon copy of Lila at that age, she was much more confident and prepared for the world around her than we ever were. After all, she grew up having never known the life we had left behind. She was her own person—smart, capable, aware, ferocious when necessary, a loner to a great extent, but kind and loving beyond imagination. She no longer even went by the name of Katie. I just still called her that from time to time. She was now Cat. Not Kat, short for Katie, but Cat. Knowing who she had become and some of the experiences that had led her to that point in her life, the name certainly fit.

So when Cat announced one day that she and eleven other teenagers were leaving Yellowstone to explore the country, we weren't totally surprised. We also shouldn't have been worried. After all, Cat was one of the most self-reliant people we had ever known. And she would be surrounded by others who had grown up in this new world.

But the fact was, we were scared. Because we all knew that there was something terrifying out there…

Part One: After Paradise

Eight Years Earlier...

Chapter 1

Ben looked down from his position on the hill at the smoke billowing from the town of Paradise, smoke that he was responsible for. He was trying to convince himself that he had done the right thing. Somehow, he had a feeling that for as long as he lived, he would strive for self-vindication. Was he rationalizing the importance of the decision, or did he really believe he was acting in everyone's best interests by destroying what might have been their only hope at ever again living a life with electricity?

The others had started back hours earlier. They had all offered to stay with him, but he had thanked them and said that he would follow. Lila, his love, and the person who knew him almost better than he knew himself, understood. This wasn't something that could be talked out, at least, not yet. Ben had to work it out for himself.

His reason for destroying the power plant had been clear at the time. People's obsession with regaining some of the life they once had was, in fact, destroying them. It wouldn't have mattered as much to Ben if the greed had been confined to the town of Paradise, but it hadn't been. It was the source of an evil that had permeated society—what was left of it anyway—well beyond the borders of Paradise. By chopping the head off the evil at the source, he had hopefully put an end to it. He wasn't naïve though. He knew it was never that simple. On the other hand, he had done what he felt must be done.

There would be a lot of anger from many of the remaining residents of Paradise. Of those, there would probably be some who would want revenge. Ben knew he would have to be on the alert for a while—maybe quite a while. For some, the anger would run deep. However, unlike the world he had once lived in, where cars, phones, and the Internet made everything happen almost instantaneously, the revenge in this case, if there was going to be any, would take time. The physical distance alone would be enough to slow the process. Paradise was many days' ride by horseback—now the primary means of transportation for most—from Ben's homestead in Yellowstone. Finding Ben's home would be another obstacle. Ben and Lila, like most others in Yellowstone, lived away from civilization to some extent. Although spread out, the population of Yellowstone—approximately two thousand at that point, was very protective of each other. Someone looking for Ben would discover it almost impossible to find a person willing to share Ben's location.

He wasn't ready to go back. He'd wait until morning. The flames had long since been extinguished, but the smoke remained. The citizens of Paradise had worked for hours putting out the fire. It was a useless gesture. Ben knew they would find nothing salvageable in the ruins. He had made sure of that.

His perch on the hill across the river was close enough that he could hear voices from time to time. He heard swearing and shouting and, occasionally, his name or his brother's name pronounced in a venomous tone. None of it bothered him. He expected it. It was only when he heard a child crying that he finally broke down himself. His tears didn't last long, but they were cathartic, and he found himself drifting off to sleep.

He awoke with a start the next morning, looking around quickly to make sure he was alone. He stretched and moved to a sheltered spot to take a last look at Paradise before getting on his way. It would take many hours to catch up to everyone, and it was time to go.

Paradise was quiet. The residents had all gone back to their homes to mourn the loss of the power and to regroup. It wasn't going to be easy to readapt. It was hard enough to lose electricity the first time, but to suddenly lose it again could send some of them over the edge. Those were the ones he felt badly for.

It was time. He had been there long enough. He worked his way down the opposite side of the hill to where Moose, his horse, was tethered. He saddled the big chestnut, climbed aboard, and started on his way.

He had a fleeting memory of the first time he had ever gotten on Moose, the previous year, the winter they stayed with the Monett community in Missouri. It had been a scary moment. He remembered how tall the horse was and how far from the ground he seemed to be, sitting so high in the saddle. Now, a little bit more than a year later, riding a horse was as natural as walking. He started on his way, following the well-defined road Lila and the rest had taken. They had probably rested at some point, so he figured he'd catch up to them by the end of the day.

It was a cool morning and the riding was pleasant. Two hours into the journey home his thoughts had finally moved on from Paradise and on to his life in Yellowstone. This trip to Paradise was unplanned. Even though he knew that Aaron, his older brother, was living there, it was too important to get settled in their new home before the onset of winter. There was much preparation to do.

The plan was to visit Paradise and connect with his brother the next spring, but all of that changed when the truck from Paradise kidnapped Katie, her friend Sophie, and Sophie's mother, while on a picnic. What started as a rescue mission became much more, culminating in the destruction of all of the Paradise vehicles and the power plant. Now Ben and Lila needed to get back and tend to their animals, generously donated by a neighbor whose stock had expanded beyond his needs. It had been a lot of work—and would continue to be—but it was all worth it. They loved where they were, the new friends they had made, and old friends they had rediscovered.

Ben was deep in thought and wasn't as aware as he should have been. Moose suddenly jerked to a halt, breaking Ben's reverie. From behind a grove of trees rode five men, each carrying a rifle pointed at Ben. They formed a semicircle in front of him

Ben recognized two of them from the night before—residents of Paradise. He was scared. He had run into countless instances of trouble over the years, and had come close to death numerous times, but there was usually a way he could wriggle out of it. This was different. These men wanted revenge, pure and simple. Why hadn't he gone back home with the rest of the group? What was his purpose in staying behind? It didn't matter now.

He was contemplating his avenues of escape—which were few to none—when the first man spoke.

"Can't believe our luck. Thought we were going to have to follow for days before we'd get our chance to kill you."

"You know that Bolli had to die," replied Ben. Bolli had been the self-appointed mayor of the town. He was a two-bit hood who had taken the name of a well-known Chicago mobster. "He was kidnapping people and bringing them to Paradise against their will. My daughter was one of those people. You don't mess with my family."

"We don't care about Bolli," said another. "You did us a favor by doing away with him. We care about the power plant. Why? Why did you do that?"

"Because you were all turning into people just like Bolli. The anger. The infighting. 'Paradise' was a misnomer if I ever heard one. Your obsession with electricity was destroying you."

"But who were you to play God?" said the first. He was a big man with a full beard and a set of the angriest eyes Ben had ever seen.

But he asked the question Ben had been struggling with all night: who was he to play God?

Finally the answer came together in his mind.

"Bolli or no Bolli, none of you fought him on his actions, which made you just as bad as he was. I was living in a town last year that your people attacked. Your people were fully prepared to kill anyone who didn't come with them. You lost any rights the minute you did that. I destroyed your power plant to prevent that from ever happening again. So no, I wasn't playing God. I was protecting my family, my friends, and good people I don't even know. I was protecting them from you. If you want to be angry, be angry at yourselves."

"Nice speech. Sounded real good."

"I thought so," replied Ben, hoping to talk long enough to scatter their attention. The plan he had was wild and would probably result in the death of Moose, which he would regret deeply. He was going to duck down beside Moose and head for the roadside trees from which the Paradise men had emerged. In the trees he'd at least have a chance.

However, as he was about to put his plan into action, a shot rang out and a puff of dirt spat up from the ground between Ben and the five men.

"Hey, Weeks," called a voice from the rocks. It was Aaron! "Why don't you and your boys lower your weapons."

"That you, Aaron? Stay out of it. This doesn't concern you."

"Well yeah, it kinda does. You see, that's my brother, and I just found him after a lot of years. It would be a real shame to lose him before we had a chance to catch up. You even attempt to hurt him and I'll mow you down. And any of you I miss—I don't ever miss, by the way—my friend Sean will get. Right Sean?"

"I might just beat you to it," came the answer from behind Ben in the rocks by the side of the road. Weeks and his crew knew that Aaron and Sean had been active-duty Marines when the event happened, and so there was no question about their marksmanship.

The five men looked at each other, then as one they lowered their weapons.

"Good choice," said Aaron.

"It's not over," said Weeks.

"It's over," said Ben. "Do what the rest of the world is doing. Learn to live off the land. Get rid of your obsession for electricity. In the long run it would have killed you."

The five looked at each other and started to walk their horses past Ben, back toward Paradise. As he passed, Weeks said in a low voice, "It's *not* over."

When they were out of sight, Aaron and Sean climbed down from the rocks.

"Thanks," said Ben. "Lucky you were there."

"It wasn't luck," said Aaron. "We know those people. We knew they wouldn't take kindly to what we did to the town. Even though you've got a reputation as some kind of savior around the country, it didn't seem the smart thing to do to leave you here alone, so we doubled back. We were up on the ridge when we saw you. And then we saw them and knew where they were going to intercept you. The rest was easy."

He gave Ben a hug. "Y'know, I saved your ass yesterday in Paradise, and now just did it again. How in the world did you survive all those years without me?"

"I had Lila to protect me."

Chapter 2

A brilliant sun shone down, warming up the day nicely as they began their long journey back to Yellowstone in silence, each reflecting on the events of the past twenty-four hours. For Ben and Aaron, it was the emotion of seeing each other after years of assuming the other was dead; for Sean and Aaron, it was best friends reunited after being apart for a couple of years; and for all three, it was the knowledge that the conflict with Weeks and his crew was probably far from over.

Sean finally broke the silence a half hour into the ride.

"We're going to have to find you a nice piece of land," he said to Aaron.

"Right down the valley from us is a beautiful spot," said Ben. "We might be willing to let you obstruct our view."

"I know the place he's talking about," said Sean. "You couldn't do much better."

"If Emily likes it, then it's sold," said Aaron. "I had a chance to talk to Lila before we turned back. She's pretty amazing."

"You don't know the half of it," replied Ben.

"When Sean and I made it back home and we were tracking your movements once we realized you might have survived the event, we went to Maiden Farms Dairy. When we determined that some sixteen-year-old girl named Lila might be with you, we figured you didn't stand a chance. Hell, I figured you couldn't even take care of yourself, much less handle having a hysterical teenage girl with you."

"That hysterical teenage girl saved my life more times than I can count. Hey, did you see a body in front of a walk-in freezer?"

"Yeah, I think so."

"He was lying right outside it," said Sean. "Or what was left of him."

"That was Richie. We owe that scumbag our lives. He thought he was punishing us by making us work in the freezer. In fact, it saved our lives. We lived. He died. Who can figure it?"

"Karma," said Sean.

"Maybe."

"I also talked to Katie," said Aaron. "She's pretty amazing as well. Unusual, to say the least."

"Lila told me she killed a man with her crossbow. I'll have to talk to her," said Ben.

"No you won't. I heard Lila discussing it with her. It's pretty obvious that Katie is different from other people. She doesn't think like we do. She doesn't see a difference between humans and animals. An animal will do whatever it needs to do to protect itself or its family. There's no remorse. And I didn't sense any of that in Katie."

"So you're saying Katie is an animal," Ben said jokingly.

"I'm saying," Aaron replied in all seriousness, "that from the little I talked to her—and to Lila—Katie relates to the animal kingdom like nobody I've ever met. I haven't seen her in action, but there was a quality that came through loud and clear."

"It's been a worry of ours," said Ben. "She spent so much of her early life in the woods without any other people around, we weren't sure how she would relate to other humans. But she seems to be doing okay."

"She'll be fine. But don't be surprised if she always relates to animals more deeply."

"You got all of that from a short talk with Katie?"

"Katie, Lila, Sean. It was all pretty obvious."

"Should I be worried about Weeks?" asked Ben, changing the subject.

"Weeks is a hothead," answered Aaron. "Normally I'd say that he'd forget about it and move on. But not this. He's on a mission. He saw all of his hopes of a return to the life he once knew die before his eyes. Yeah, I'd be worried. Just be extra careful for a while."

"His life wasn't going to return to what it used to be."

"Of course not," said Sean. "But at least he had the means to pretend that it was. Now he doesn't have that."

"Did I make a mistake?" asked Ben.

The other two were silent for a moment.

"No," Sean finally said. "Brittany and I left because we didn't like what was happening there—and that was even before Marco Bolli took over. The town was destined for failure. You just hastened its demise a bit."

*****

They reached the others that evening. They were camped on the shores of a large, pristine lake. Ben never failed to notice that, with each passing year after the event, everything seemed cleaner—the water, the air, and the smell. He was convinced that the earth was repairing itself.

"Daddy!" Katie was running toward him, arms outstretched. She jumped into his arms and hugged him tightly.

"Hi Kiddo. I've missed you."

He put Katie down as Lila approached. They sank into each other's arms, then kissed deeply.

"Good to have you back," she said. He was sure there was a double meaning there.

"Good to be back, thanks to Aaron and Sean." He told her the story of Weeks and his crew.

"How many times have we almost lost each other?" she asked.

"More than I can count," Ben answered. "We live a charmed life."

"Until we don't," said Lila. "We need to be extra careful. I agree with Aaron and Sean, he's not done trying to exact his revenge."

Ben held Lila away from his body and stared at her.

"God, you're beautiful."

When she smiled, the side of her mouth crinkled slightly. It was the smile that attracted Ben to her so long ago as teenagers. Back then she was pleasant-looking, but not a beauty. That was something that developed as she aged. Now, with her shiny black hair rolling over her shoulder blades, and the matching black eyepatch covering her useless right eye—the result of an accident a few years earlier—he wondered how he could have been so lucky as to greet the new world with someone as beautiful and as courageous as Lila by his side.

*****

That night, Ben, Lila, Sean, Aaron, and Emily, Aaron's tall, dark, schoolteacher companion, originally from Haiti, sat by a campfire eating fish. Sean's wife Brittany and their children were back in Yellowstone. Katie had fallen asleep with Ralph the dog.

"So tell us about Yellowstone," said Aaron.

"It's so different from Paradise, it will make your head spin," said Sean. "We have a small town—Rock Creek—but it's used mostly as a gathering place for most of the families. Brittany and I live in the town, with maybe fifty other families, but the rest, like Ben and Lila, live in the hills. We have a doctor and a dentist, a vet, a church, a school—we only have one teacher and our child population is growing, so your skills will be deeply appreciated, Emily—and a general store of sorts that I run. I go on scavenging missions to bring things back that people might need. There's no cost, of course, since we don't have money. People take what they need, and offer me their skills in return, whenever I have need of them. I don't take as many scavenging trips as I used to, but every once in a while I'll fire up the old horse and buggy and venture out. We even have a small restaurant, but I heard them say the other day that they will probably close it. There's no real need for it. I think it was an homage of sorts to the way things used to be, but the fact is, things aren't the way they used to be, and there's no reason to pretend."

"The loosely structured barter system we have in place seems to work well and I'm not sure we'll ever change that," continued Sean. "The people are supportive of each other, and that's why it works. Some people prefer to be left alone and some want to be involved in everything. But when it comes down to it, we can count on everybody when the chips are down. Lifestyles aren't a concern. Hell, we have a brother and sister living together who, I think, over the years have become more than just siblings. Kinda creepy, if you ask me, but in this new world, who's to judge? We all had to do whatever it took to survive. We try to have weekly activities in town—cook-outs, bingo, things for the kids, that sort of stuff. We even have a theatre group. One of our residents used to direct community plays. Brittany has gotten involved. The first show is next month. In short, living in Yellowstone is like living in heaven."

"Sounds it," said Aaron. "Any troublemakers?"

"We've had a few, but they are all gone. We won't put up with that kind of shit. We've worked too hard to make this a success." He looked at Ben. "I wouldn't be surprised to see some Paradise refugees show up in the near future. Without the electricity, there is little to keep them there. It's going to continue to be an ugly place until they can clean house of the bad apples. I think some will just choose to leave rather than having to confront the situation. We might have some tough decisions to make. A lot of them will be coming with chips on their shoulders ... with a lot of anger."

"Then they don't stay. Simple as that," said one of the Yellowstone men standing on the outskirts of the conversation. "We make it clear to them from day one what is expected. They cause trouble, they leave. That's how we've done it from the beginning. We're not going to change it now."

The conversation eventually tailed off, with everyone finding a quiet place to bed down for the night. Ben picked up Katie and brought her to a secluded spot Lila had picked out. Two of the men volunteered to take turns standing guard.

When Katie was again settled, Ben and Lila got under the blankets and held each other.

"Have you made peace with yourself?" Lila asked.

"To a degree. I'll never know if what I did was morally right, but it was what I had to do. We live in a world where we live and die by our decisions, and we don't always have the luxury of time to debate whether it's a right or wrong choice. I did what I had to do. Some people will benefit by the decision and some might be hurt by it. I have no control over that. We went there to save our daughter, and as I said to Weeks, 'You don't mess with my family.' So, yes, I guess I have made peace with myself."

"Good." Lila put her arms around Ben and squeezed him tightly. Within minutes, they were naked and quietly making love.

Chapter 3

Life for all of us settled down as preparations were made for the winter. Still a couple of months away, it was never too early to start, considering the unpredictable weather. This was going to be my family's first winter in Yellowstone, but it couldn't be any worse than some of the winters we experienced in the Smoky Mountains, or the violent blizzards our one winter in Monett.

Aaron and Emily loved the spot I suggested, and their house was built in record time with the help of almost twenty neighbors. They lived only a half mile down the valley from us. It was still mind-boggling to me that my brother was back in my life. Despite him being six years older, we were always close. But I always knew that he felt I couldn't take care of myself. And like any big brother, he wasn't afraid to tell me. It was a new world though. He was always going to rag on me, but now it would be with respect. I was not the little brother he left so many years ago when he joined the Marines. We both knew we were going to enjoy getting to know each other again.

The first of the expected Paradise refugees arrived in the late fall—not an intelligent decision on their part with winter coming on. Long before we showed up, the Yellowstone community had developed a simple interview process for potential residents. Those with children were almost always accepted, but the rest had to submit to the questions. Only a few had ever failed the interview. Not so with the Paradise group. Of the sixty former Paradise residents seeking to relocate to Yellowstone, five were denied. Sean was on the board who interviewed them and said that those five displayed a transparent anger toward the Yellowstone residents, and toward me in particular. Sean said it wasn't easy to deny them entry into the community, especially with winter not far off, but if they made an exception to the standards once, it would be the beginning of the end. Needless to say, those five were not happy and threatened all kinds of nasty things. Sean told them to go pound sand. At over six feet tall and more than 200 pounds—most of it muscle—few people chose to argue with Sean.

Nothing had been heard from Weeks and his crew, but I wasn't fooled. He was a man with a deep grudge, and sooner or later he'd try to do something about it. I just hoped I'd be ready when the time came.

The winter was relatively mild, a nice treat for Ben and Lila, who had experienced one harsh winter after another ever since the event. It was still cold and there was plenty of snow, but there were few violent storms. Travel was still possible, which made the winter bearable. Katie was able to get to school most days, and Ben and Lila worked on finishing the inside of the house and the barn. Ben would go out hunting once or twice a week, usually bringing back enough to share with some of the older people—most of whom lived in town.

In March, elections were held and Lila was elected to the Yellowstone Board, a group of seven who worked to drive the future of Yellowstone and Rock Creek. At first she wasn't going to put her name in the hat, but feedback from friends and neighbors convinced her to give it a try.

Whereas Ben preferred to stay in the background, the respect and admiration for Lila's leadership skills had grown rapidly from the moment they arrived. Despite her youth—although in the new world, the mid-20s was no longer a drawback for respect—she possessed a common sense and strength that was hard to find.

*****

By April the snow was beginning to melt, the streams were rushing, and there was a hint of spring in the air. Ben was ten miles down the valley on a hunting expedition, hoping to bring back a buck to share with neighbors. He often hunted with Aaron, but on this day Aaron was nursing a bad cold, so Ben went on his own. He didn't mind. He loved the peace he felt every time he took one of his trips. For a while, during his early trips, he would think about his old life back in Massachusetts and how different and more fulfilling this was. Besides the lack of noise, everything was cleaner—the air, the water, and even his very being. He missed some things from his old life, like baseball, and even some of his favorite TV shows, not to mention his computer and iPad. But in so many other ways this life couldn't get any better. But those were in the early days. He rarely thought of those things now. Now he just appreciated the life he had.

*****

He never heard the shot, but he cried out in pain as something hot hit him in the leg. The unexpectedness of it caused him to fall from his horse. He hit the soggy ground face-first, momentarily stunned. And then he heard it. A gunshot. Then another. Moose whinnied as a bullet grazed his hind quarters. They were shooting at his horse! Instead of taking off, Moose stayed with Ben.

Ben reached up and tried to pull his rifle from its scabbard attached to his saddle, but Moose moved. He was already too exposed, so he slapped Moose hard on the butt and yelled at him to go.

"Get out of here. Go, go, go, go!"

The horse took off at a gallop, heading back the way they had come. A couple more shots followed Moose up the trail, then they tapered off. Moose had made it!

Ben looked around quickly and spied a small cluster of rocks less than fifty feet away. He hobbled to them, his leg killing him. The bullet had hit him in the thigh and he didn't think it had done any major damage, but it hurt like hell. He needed to reach the rocks and try to put something on the wound.

The dirt kicked up next to his foot and he heard a gunshot. A second shot, then a third. He didn't have time to think, he just needed to make it to the safety of the rocks. When he got within a few yards, he fell to the ground and crawled the rest of the way. He didn't know if it made him safer, but it felt that way. He rose to his knees and dove the final yard just as a bullet tugged at his coat. He was safe for the moment.

The shooting momentarily stopped, their target now invisible. After a quick look over the rocks, Ben checked his wound. His jeans were soaked with blood. He took off his holster, unbuckled his belt and pulled his pants down to his knees. The leg was ugly, but mostly because of the blood. He took off his coat, outer shirt, and t-shirt, and wiped the blood off with the t-shirt. It wasn't too bad—a small smooth entry hole and a slightly larger, more ragged, exit. The blood was flowing, but not dangerously so. He could tell the bullet hadn't hit an artery. He wrapped the t-shirt tightly around the wound and tied it in a knot, all the while grimacing in pain. He gingerly pulled up his pants and buckled his belt. For comfort purposes, he set the holster and gun down next to him. The chill in the air was beginning to sink into his bones, so he quickly put on his outer shirt and coat, zipping the coat to the top.

It was time to take stock of his situation. It wasn't good. Both his crossbow and M-16 were still on Moose—the crossbow he used for hunting and the M-16 for protection—which left him with his Sig .40 caliber pistol, the same one he had been using since right after the event. The magazine held ten rounds, and he only had the one magazine. The two spare magazines were in his saddlebags, now probably a mile away. Ten rounds wouldn't get him very far, and the pistol was only effective at close range. If his attackers stayed in the woods, his gun was useless.

A couple of ineffective shots hit the rocks, and then there was once again silence. It would do no good to fire back. He was going to have to make each shot count. He wasn't sure how many men were out there. From the sounds of the guns, he knew there had to be at least three, but possibly more. Moose would eventually find his way home and it wouldn't take Lila more than an hour to gather up enough bodies for a rescue party. Realistically though, it could be several hours before they arrived—assuming Moose went directly home and assuming they had any idea where he was. Luckily, Ben was near the trail and hadn't ventured deep into the woods. At least he now had a general time frame—for whatever good that would do him.

He assumed Weeks was leading the group. Aaron had filled him in on Weeks. It was kind of a sad story—something the new world was full of. Like so many others, he had lost his family in the event, and had spent a couple of years wandering. He drifted from one community to another, finally meeting a woman named Ada near Charlotte, North Carolina. Although there was no great love between them, there was companionship. They figured it was the best they were going to get. They stayed together for a year or so, until the plague hit. No one seemed to know what the plague was—one rumor had it originating from an abandoned biological testing facility—but it didn't need a name. It killed all it infected—including Ada. Weeks somehow avoided catching the plague and immediately headed west. Again he met a woman, and again she died, this time a long horrible ordeal at the hands of bandits, resulting in a painful death that a bound Weeks had to witness. Somehow, he managed to escape, but he went back and slaughtered the bandits, making sure each died a slow, painful death. Eventually making it to Paradise, Weeks had finally found a little peace—until Ben destroyed the power plant, that is. Aaron had made it clear to Ben that Weeks wasn't someone to be trifled with. He was an angry man and someone who had known a lot of violence. If Ben ran across him again, he would have to be prepared to fight to the death.

Assuming it was Weeks, he and his crew wouldn't want to

wait hours. They would also be as aware as Ben that if Ben's horse found his way home, a rescue attempt would be made. Weeks would want to do the deed and get out of there long before having to face a well-armed force.

Would that be such a bad thing for Ben? What if he could lure them into the open? It would give him a fighting chance with them closer.

"Ben! We know you're alive," came Weeks's voice from the trees. "We also know you're wounded. You don't have your rifle. Maybe if you run for the trees on the other side, you'll have a chance. If not, we can wait. You'll eventually pass out from loss of blood. Your choices don't look so hot—sort of like the choice you gave us in Paradise."

Ben was pretty sure he wouldn't pass out. He had the wound tightly wrapped and he was sure he wasn't losing any more blood. Weeks's problem was that if he couldn't see Ben, he had no idea if he was unconscious. Ben was determined to keep it that way. There was no way he could see the men in the woods without them seeing him, so he was going to have to rely on sound. He was pretty sure he'd be able to hear them coming. After all, these were Paradise men, used to living in town with—up until recently—some modern conveniences. They had no feel for nature. They'd make plenty of noise. Of that, Ben had no doubt. He just had to hunker down and wait.

An hour passed, and then two. Every once in a while a bullet would sting the top of the rocks, but he was safe as long as he stayed low. There was the occasional taunt from the edge of the woods, but eventually both the talking and the shooting subsided. Ben knew what they were thinking: Was Ben alive? Conscious? Should they go check it out? Knowing that help was eventually going to find its way there, time was becoming an issue. Every once in a while, he thought he heard arguing. Chances were, some of them wanted to check on Ben and some probably just wanted to leave altogether.

At one point he almost gave himself away when he developed a major cramp in his foot. He came close to jumping up and walking it off, but if he did that, it would be the last walking he'd ever do. As painful as it was, he tried working it out from a prone position, stretching until it finally subsided.

Ben had been behind the rocks for almost three hours when he heard the sound of a pebble being kicked. It was faint, but it was the sound he'd been waiting for. He had to give them credit, they had been more patient than he figured they'd be. Whoever had kicked the pebble probably wasn't even aware of it, but Ben heard it and picked up his gun.

Another sound. This time from off to his right. That meant there was probably someone else coming up on his left. They were planning to surround him. He had to make a decision quickly. If he waited for them to reach him, he could get them at almost point-blank range. But then again, they'd be point-blank range from him, and there were more of them. Or, he could shoot now and still have the cover of the rocks. It was a no-brainer.

He rolled over onto his stomach and peeked around the right side of the rocks. His target was only 20 feet away, stepping carefully. Ben fired twice and the man went down. Rolling to his left, he saw the second man, now running toward him. Again, Ben fired twice, and again, the man went down. Ben looked over the top of the rocks. There were three others. It was the same five who had stopped him that day on the trail.

Aware that he only had six bullets left, he took a quick shot at the closest man, who was about 25 feet away, and missed. His second shot brought him down.

Four bullets and two men! They were moving quickly now, first to the left, then to the right, but closing in on Ben in the process. One of them was Weeks. Ben took two shots and missed with both. The other man slipped and fell to the ground, momentarily dazed. Ben took aim and shot, hitting the man in the leg. He cried out and dropped his rifle. Ben swung his gun back in the direction of Weeks, but the man was almost upon him. He fired and heard Weeks grunt. The bullet had struck him in the side, but hadn't stopped him. Weeks saw the slide retract on Ben's gun and knew it was empty. He shot and missed while running, then landed on Ben like a block of cement, swinging wildly at him with his fists.

Later on, when Ben had time to reflect, he wondered why Weeks had done that. He could have stopped, aimed his pistol, and put an end to Ben once and for all. But he chose to physically attack him. It was Lila who cleared it up for Ben. She explained that Weeks's anger was so all-consuming, it was his only option. Shooting Ben would have ended it physically, but not emotionally. He had to feel Ben's pain.

Ben, already weakened by his wound, didn't stand a chance against Weeks. Even though the man was also wounded, he was bigger and stronger than Ben. And he had anger on his side, an out of control rage that made him almost invincible. Weeks sat on Ben's stomach, pounding him in the neck and face, all the while screaming at him. In his haze, Ben almost thought Weeks was crying as he slugged away.

Ben was losing consciousness. He knew that the moment

he did, he was a dead man. Weeks would keep on pounding until there was no life left in Ben's body. Ben grabbed at the man's hips and tried to push him off, to no avail. He no longer had the strength.

But then he felt it. Weeks had a knife sheath on his belt. Ben felt for the knife and grabbed hold of the hilt. It was a hunting knife, at least six inches long. He tried to pull it out, but something was holding it. A leather thong was fastened across the top of it to keep it from popping out of the sheath while he rode his horse.

The blows were slowing down and were landing with less of an impact. It didn't matter. Weeks had done his job. Ben was almost gone. But he couldn't let it end this way, not after all he'd been through. He fumbled with the piece of leather and felt it pull free. With his remaining strength, he yanked the knife from its case, reached his arm back, and then, with all the strength he could muster, drove it into the man's side.

Weeks let out a scream and then collapsed on top of Ben.

The next thing Ben knew, it was dark out, and so cold. No, there were lights, lots of lights. He could feel Weeks being pulled off of him and he could hear Lila's voice. He didn't know what she was saying, but he knew she was there. He heard other voices as well—Aaron's ... but wasn't he sick? And then he heard nothing at all.

*****

It took a couple of months for Ben to heal from his wounds, the bullet wound being the least of the injuries. Weeks had done quite the job on Ben's face, to the point where the doctor was afraid Ben might suffer from brain damage. Those fears were unfounded, however, and the doctor eventually cleared him—with the remark that Ben was very, very lucky.

Ben didn't feel lucky. He had a broken nose, three chipped teeth, bruises to the throat that made swallowing painful for many days, and permanent hearing loss in one ear.

From Lila and Aaron, he got the full story. Moose did eventually make it home. Seeing not just the riderless horse, but Ben's weapons still on the horse, Lila knew something severe had happened to Ben. She quickly rode into town and rounded up as many people as she could, ending up with thirteen men and three women. She left Katie with Brittany and had her posse, including Sean and the doctor, ready in less than an hour. On their way they stopped at Aaron's house and pulled him out of bed, knowing he'd never forgive them if he wasn't part of the rescue party.

The lone clue they had to his whereabouts was him having told Lila that he was going further down the trail that day, probably to the ten to twelve mile mark. They followed the well-used trail hoping he hadn't strayed too far from it. Night came, but that didn't deter them. Using hand-cranked rechargeable flashlights that Sean had discovered on one of his scavenging trips, they continued on their way. They would have missed him entirely if they hadn't run across the horses belonging to Weeks and his crew, still tied in the woods beside the trail. From there, it wasn't hard to find him, Weeks's dead body still draped over him.

Ben's last-second desperation thrust of the knife had been a lucky hit. It passed between two ribs and caught Weeks's heart from the side. Death came within seconds. By the doctor's best guess, Ben had been lying under Weeks for at least three hours. Besides Weeks, two of the other men were also dead, one of whom, the doctor calculated, had probably taken a couple of hours to die. The two remaining men were taken to the doctor's office, where he nursed them back to health. The debate was lively as to what to do with them, but it was finally decided that they were swayed by Weeks's quest for vengeance more than anger at Ben on their own part. When they were healthy, they were let go with the threat that if either one of them was spotted anywhere near Yellowstone, he would be hunted down and killed. They both promised to go back to Paradise and never head in the direction of Yellowstone again.

Of course, Ben's reputation—built so many years earlier with Lila after the event—which had finally begun to fade into the background, was once again revived, much to his chagrin. It was a classic story: A lone man, a bullet wound in his leg and a single pistol, trapped out in the open behind a small pile of rocks against a force of five (sometimes ten, a few times even fifteen in the retellings—although how he could kill fifteen men with ten bullets was beyond Ben's comprehension). Somehow in the story he is able to kill all five (in none of the retellings do any of the men survive), and although near death himself, he survives to fight again another day.

All Ben could hope for was that the story would eventually die out.

Chapter 4

While Ben was recuperating, Lila and Katie took over most of the hunting. Katie loved animals, but understood the need for hunting from spending her life watching how the animals interacted with each other. The animals hunted only to survive, and that made sense to her. When she had to kill an animal for food, she always thanked it for giving up its life for them. Even at her young age, she had become an excellent shot with a rifle, a pistol, and her small crossbow.

They were about three miles from the house, walking through the forest. They had left their horses at home. The horses would have only telegraphed their presence to the wildlife around them. Besides, they were only hunting birds that day—wild turkeys or quail. They weren't going after anything heavy like a deer.

Truth be told, if they came back empty-handed, they wouldn't have been disappointed. They loved the time they spent together. They talked and collected edible plants, and Lila would quiz Katie on the names of different plants and animals. Lila was always amazed at how much more life Katie had than Lila had had at the same age. Besides all of the distractions kids had when she was young, Lila had also had to deal with parents who held her back. Katie had none of that. The hills, mountains, forests, and valleys were her playground, and although she didn't spend a lot of time with other children, she never felt deprived. In fact, she preferred it that way.

On this day, the hunting was poor. They saw very few animals of any kind, something Lila found odd.

"They're scared," said Katie, when Lila made mention of it.

"Scared of what? Us?"

"No. They're not afraid of us. Something else."

Lila knew better than to dismiss anything Katie said when it came to animals. Immediately her senses went on high alert.

"What do you think it is?"

"Something big. A bear or a big cat."

They hadn't yet run across a mountain lion in their time in Yellowstone, but had seen numerous bears from a distance. The black bears were large, but nothing compared to the one grizzly bear they once saw. Even from a half mile away, it looked enormous. Nick and Jason had told them that grizzlies were flourishing. The males ranged in weight from 600-900 pounds, but Nick had seen one that he said had to weigh close to 1200 pounds. Nick said the monster was standing next to a tree and was almost ten feet tall—as tall as the tree itself.

They walked a while longer, until Katie suddenly stopped and said, "We need to go home."

"Why? Are you feeling okay?"

"It's wrong."

"What's wrong?"

"Everything. The air. It feels funny. My hair, I think it's standing up. Mommy, we have to go, now."

Lila knew better than to question her daughter's feelings.

"Okay, let's go home now."

"It's too late."

"What?"

"It's too late. We can't go that way." She put her face in the air for just a moment. "This way."

Lila followed her daughter unquestioningly as they ventured deeper into the woods.

"What is it?

"Bad. Faster mommy."

And then Lila heard it and felt her heart almost skip a beat. It was a crashing in the brush behind them and a grunting—a horrifying grunting. Katie had sensed an animal, but Lila knew now that it wasn't just any animal. It was a grizzly bear. Any grizzly would be a big one, but she sensed, mostly based on Katie's feelings, that this wasn't any ordinary grizzly. This was a true monster.

They had almost no time. They weren't talking minutes, but seconds. It was time for Lila to take over. To their left was a rocky hill, covered with boulders and tall trees. There had to be a hiding place. She took Katie's hand and started to run.

From behind them they heard the heavy pounding of the bear barreling through bushes. Lila hadn't encountered an animal this aggressive since the early days after the event, when so many of the animals seemed to have had their brains scrambled. This was nothing more than an aggressive animal—and they were its prey. Lila knew she could stand and fight, but her gun was no match for a grizzly bear. She needed something bigger and more powerful. She might eventually kill the beast, but most likely, she would be dead before she got off even a couple of shots.

They needed a tree. A strong, thick tree. But then, how would they climb it? Lila knew that bears climbed trees, but she was hoping that the sheer size of this one might prevent him from climbing.

He was still behind them, crashing through the underbrush, but hadn't yet shown himself. They couldn't make it much farther. Katie, with her short legs, had reached her limit. And then Lila saw it. The perfect tree! It was tall and substantial. The trunk was fat and smooth. There were no handholds, but next to it was a rock. By standing on the rock and holding Katie up, her daughter could reach some of the smaller branches and pull herself up. Lila could then jump up from the rock and grab hold of the branches.

She scooped up Katie and ran to the rock. She held her up to the tree and said, "Grab the branches and pull yourself up. Just keep going up as far as you can."

Lila was exhausted and Katie was dead weight, but somehow she lifted her daughter to her shoulders. Katie stood on Lila's shoulders and reached up, snagging a branch. Lila pushed and Katie was able to get a foot secure. From there it was easy and Katie scrambled up a few feet.

"Come on, mommy. Your turn." She looked into the woods. "He's coming. Hurry."

Too late!

The bear emerged from the brush with a roar. Facing Lila, he stopped and raised himself on his hind legs to his full height. He had to be twelve feet tall. Lila wondered if Katie was high enough in the tree. She knew there was no way she could make it up in time before the animal attacked.

"I'm not going to move," she whispered up to Katie. She

was pretty sure that was the thing to do when confronted by a wild animal.

"He's going to attack anyway," her daughter replied. Lila wondered how she could be so calm.

The bear roared again, and as he did, from her place on the branch, Katie raised her crossbow, pulled the trigger, and let the arrow fly. It went straight into the bear's open mouth.

The bear let out an otherworldly scream and pawed at the arrow.

"Now Mommy," yelled Katie. Lila jumped. The rifle on her back was impeding her jump, so she quickly slid the strap over her head and passed the rifle up to Katie, who had come down a couple branches to help if she could. Lila jumped again, this time barely grabbing the branch. But it was enough of a grip. She scrambled up the trunk until she was in a secure spot. But they weren't high enough.

"Keep moving up. He can reach us here."

The bear, meanwhile, had grabbed hold of the arrow and managed to pull it out of his mouth. Now he leapt for the tree and swatted at Lila, who was still the closest to the ground. But Lila had made it just beyond his reach. She kept climbing. The branches were strong and the two of them climbed as high as they could, well out of the reach of the bear.

"Hopefully he won't climb up here," she said.

"He won't," said Katie. "He's too big."

Lila understood what her daughter meant. It was a lot of weight to carry around, and climbing a tree wouldn't be easy. Instead, the bear sat at the bottom of the tree and looked up at them. He was picking at his mouth where the arrow had gone in. It would hurt, but Lila was sure it had done him little harm.

He gave another roar to let them know he was thinking about them, then settled down at the base of the tree. He wasn't going anywhere. Lila retrieved her rifle from Katie.

"It doesn't look like he's going anywhere anytime soon."

"I'm comfortable," said Katie.

And then Lila began to laugh. It was relief pouring out. She also had to laugh because Katie could sound so adult at times.

When she was done, she looked at the rifle in her hand—the hand was shaking—and down at the bear. "I suppose I could start pumping bullets into him." But even as she said it, she knew she could only do it as a last resort. To kill an animal so majestic—even one that wanted her for dinner—just seemed wrong. No, they were just going to have to wait.

"You can't kill him, Mom." The "adult" Katie, now talking.

"Way ahead of you."

But Lila was worried. They could probably wait out the bear overnight. Eventually he would leave, but when they came down from the tree, would he be lurking in the woods waiting for them?

The bear grunted and stood up on his hind legs. He looked at Lila and Katie high up in the branches and roared. He stood up on the rock and tried to climb the tree. Lila could see blood soaking the fur around his mouth. She knew he had to be in a lot of pain. He was also pissed.

Lila put her rifle to her shoulder. A few bullets to the head would probably kill him. If he was a rogue bear, she would probably be doing people a favor by killing him. And yet, this was his land more than it was theirs. What right did she have to kill him? They could cut out the choice bits of meat, but they already had a good supply of meat. His fur would make a fine blanket or rug, but they had blankets and rugs, as did most of their neighbors.

She came to her decision. She would only kill him—or more realistically, try to kill him—if he posed a further threat to them.

"Are you okay up there?" she asked Katie, who was about ten feet higher than Lila.

"I'm good." Once more, Katie's comfort in the wild amazed Lila. She tried to imagine herself at the age of eight or nine in the same situation. She would have cried her eyes out. She had a funny memory of a camping trip she once took with some relatives—oh, how long ago that seemed. Another life altogether. They were all upset because they didn't have any Wi-Fi connections for their iPads. They spent the evening sitting around a bonfire eating Kentucky Fried Chicken and looking over the shoulder of the one person who had downloaded a movie to his iPad. Definitely another life.

Her attention was brought back to the bear, who roared again and gave up his attempts to climb the tree. The bear and the tree just weren't the right fit. He settled down and licked his lips. He looked up at Lila. She could have sworn he gave her a dirty look. He licked his claws—his massive claws. One swipe would take her head off. She shuddered at the thought of how close she had come to dying. Katie, who didn't want to kill the bear, had no trouble shooting the arrow into his mouth. Again, her daughter's practical side came out. Her love of animals mattered little in that case. A bear was attacking her mother and she had to stop him. Now that he was stopped, she wanted him to live.

Hours later they were still in the tree. The grizzly appeared to have fallen asleep at the base of the tree, but they knew better. Toward dark, the bear suddenly got up on his hind legs and rubbed his back on the tree, then moved into the woods. Lila remembered Nick and Jason saying that grizzly males marked their territory by rubbing the trees.

Lila looked at Katie.

"He'll be back," said her daughter. Then she said, "I have to pee ... really bad."

So did Lila. Suddenly, she had an idea. She adjusted herself on her branch and undid her belt, carefully sliding her pants down to her thighs. With her naked butt hanging over the branch, she peed down the side of the tree.

As she peed, she said to Katie, "He was marking his spot. I wonder how happy he'll be to find that we marked it too."

Katie's face lit up. She climbed down to a branch on the opposite side of the tree, pulled her pants down and copied her mother, soaking that side of the tree with pee.

Soon after that, the bear returned, grunting and snuffling as he walked. Lila couldn't help admiring what a magnificent animal he was. At the same time, she was more than happy to keep her distance.

As the bear approached the tree, he was bothered and shook his head. He came closer, appearing to smell the tree. He wasn't happy at all and shook his head some more. He looked up at Lila one more time, then sauntered into the woods.

"He's not coming back," said Katie.

Lila was pretty proud of herself and was tempted to climb down, but it was getting dark.

A search party would be out looking for them soon. Ben wouldn't wait until morning to send help. She and Katie were better off staying right where they were. If no one had come by morning, they could leave.

Two hours later, they heard a gunshot. Lila pointed her rifle in the air and fired off a round. A few minutes later she saw flashlights. She pulled hers out, cranked it up, and pointed it in the direction of the others. The crank flashlights weren't as powerful as the battery flashlights she grew up with, but at this point in time, all traditional batteries had lost their charge. She shot one more round to keep them coming in the right direction. They saw her light and she could hear the sounds of horses coming up the trail. A few minutes later, Aaron, Emily, and Sean crowded around the bottom of the tree. She was glad to see that Ben stayed home, given his healing injuries, although it was probably killing him to do so.

"Got lost, did we?" asked Aaron with a chuckle.

"Long story," said Lila, helping Katie down.

Sean pointed his flashlight at the base of the tree and saw blood patches and Katie's bloody arrow.

"But a good one, I bet," he said.

Lila and Katie, now on the backs of the horses, just looked at each other and smiled.

*****

The bear was spotted from time to time over the next couple of years. It stayed away from the Yellowstone settlement, and the Yellowstone residents, in turn, stayed far away from the bear if they sensed his presence. The couple of times people ran across him, he was just as aggressive as he had been with Lila and Katie. Jason, the veterinarian, said it was the largest bear he had ever seen, and had no explanation for the bear's ornery behavior. His only theory was that the bear was alive at the time of the event, and like so many other large mammals, his brain got a little fried.

The bear became somewhat of a legend with his occasional appearances, prompting Ben to call it Bigfoot, after the urban legends that he remembered from childhood. Katie couldn't understand the name.

"Of course his feet are big, Daddy. It's because he is big. He couldn't have small feet."

Ben decided that it would be better to wait until Katie, who tended to think literally, was older before trying to explain the name and tell the story.

The Bigfoot sightings stopped about three years after Lila and Katie's encounter. No one knew what happened to the bear, whether he just moved on or he died. Curiously, he was missed by all in the Yellowstone community, with the possible exception of Lila and Katie.

Chapter 5

By the time Katie was ten, she was already traveling far and wide by herself, when she wasn't in school. Despite being a stellar student, with interests that ranged from science to history, school bored her. She couldn't wait for the school day to end so she could mount Scooby and go exploring. Ben and Lila realized early on that Katie was different, and as such, normal rules didn't apply to her. She knew not to do anything foolish—she had grown up in a world where a poor decision could be deadly. She was always home before it got dark and always did her homework after dinner. If she was asked to come home right after school to do chores, she complied enthusiastically. In many ways, she seemed like a perfect child.

But Ben and Lila were worried. Katie got along with just about everybody and had many friends, which pleased them, but she had no close friends. There was no special person in her life. Her special friends were her horse Scooby and her dog Ralph, although Ralph was getting older and spent more time around the house and less time taking trips with Katie. Katie had an adventurous streak that left her little time to make normal friends. If they weren't into exploring nature, she didn't seem to see the point in spending time with them.

When she was younger and they were new to Yellowstone, she had formed a strong bond with Sophie, a neighbor who was the same age as Katie. When Katie was kidnapped by the Paradise crowd, Sophie and her mother were captured along with her. But while Katie showed a streak of bravery—despite being scared—Sophie spent much of her time in a state of panic. After Paradise, Katie spent less and less time with Sophie, the friendship eventually fading away. Brenda, Sophie's mother, couldn't understand Katie's pulling away from the friendship, but Ben and Lila knew. Katie didn't understand—and as a result, couldn't respect—the absence of courage. Subconsciously, she had nothing left in common with Sophie.

Ben and Lila had many talks about their daughter, always coming to pretty much the same conclusion each time: she was who she was, and there was nothing they could do to change that. Not that they necessarily wanted to change her. To do so would be to trap and constrict her. Both of them had dealt with numerous constraints as children and understood that, and in this new world, it was the last thing they would want to do to Katie.

Although Katie never verbalized it, she found animals to be much more interesting than humans. And the animals seemed to sense it. She could get within feet of a deer before it took flight—and occasionally even found one that would let her touch it.

While she carried a rifle and pistol for protection when she rode and was an excellent shot, she rarely used either. She found the noise unnatural in the wild. She used Ben's old pistol crossbow, and was just waiting for the day when she would be strong enough to manage a full-sized crossbow.

*****

The day she met the cat, her life changed forever.

It was a Saturday (at least, according to the calendar Nick had come up with based on lunar activity) and she had the day free to explore. She went down the valley three or four miles, far past her Uncle Aaron's property, to a pine forest she often visited. A fast-running stream originating somewhere in the distant high mountains ran along the edge of the forest. A few months earlier she had found a large flat rock at the edge of the stream, and it was perfect for daydreaming and animal watching.

This day was no different. She had her eyes closed, listening to the running water next to her and the crying birds high above in the trees. She had dozed off and almost missed it. Maybe it was Scooby's fussing in the woods where he was tied, or maybe it was the squeaking coming from across the stream—an unfamiliar sound. She woke with a start. Across the water on the opposite bank and fifty feet upstream was a mountain lion with three small cubs.

Despite often seeing tracks of the big cats and sometimes hearing a cry in the woods, she had never actually seen a mountain lion. She was amazed at its size; its sleek and muscular body was like nothing she had ever seen. Fascinated by the scene playing out before her, she remained perfectly still, so as not to disturb the family outing upstream. If the big cat knew Katie was there, she gave no indication of it. Katie was often accepted by the animals as just part of the backdrop of nature.

The three cubs were playing and the mother was doing her best to round them up. She was probably teaching them something, but Katie wasn't sure exactly what. The cubs were small, maybe two feet long, and they were rolling around, having the time of their lives. Katie watched for the longest time. The mother had long since given up trying to teach them anything and was now lying quietly watching them frolic.

Katie was momentarily distracted by an eagle overhead when she heard a screech. She looked back to see one of the lions in the water. Their wrestling had gotten them too close to the edge of the stream and one had gone over the edge. The mother leapt up and with a powerful swipe knocked the remaining two cubs several yards from the edge. In a second she was racing downstream, trying to catch up with the young cub, who was trying to keep its head above the swirling water.

The stream wasn't rushing at a great speed, but the current was still strong—much too strong for the cub. Katie could immediately see that the cub was going to die if she didn't do something. The mother was panicking, keeping abreast of her cub, but helpless to do anything about it.

Katie jumped off the rock and ran to Scooby, quickly untying his reins from the branch. She was in the saddle in a matter of seconds. The startled horse reacted to her touch and shot off downstream. Katie kept an eye on both the mother and the cub, hoping to get ahead of them and intercept the cub before it drowned. She looked ahead and saw the spot about a hundred and fifty feet away. A rock jutted out into the stream. If she could reach it in time, she could maybe grab the cub as he went by.

She was now ahead of both lions, but she'd have to go even faster to reach the rock and put herself into position in time to intercept the cub. Scooby seemed to sense the need for speed and picked up his pace. When they reached the rock, Katie reined Scooby in, almost sailing over his head. She jumped off the horse and hit the ground and rolled, momentarily dazed. But she quickly regained her senses and rushed to the rock. She made it with seconds to spare. She braced herself as best she could. The cub was small, but she knew it would still be heavy as she tried to pluck it from the water.

It was almost there. It had stopped struggling, but Katie hoped it was just exhausted, not dead. Almost … almost. Now! Katie reached out and grabbed the waterlogged animal. The force of the current almost pulled her off the rock, but she flopped to her belly and somehow managed to stay on the rock.

She pulled the lion cub to her chest and held on. She felt its heart beating. He was alive, but his energy was totally spent. She laid there for a minute, catching her breath. Then she looked up to see the mother lion sitting on the other side of the stream watching her warily. Katie stood up, holding the cub. She instinctively knew that what she was about to do was dangerous, but she was willing to take the chance.

She stepped into the water. The current was strong, but the water only came to her knees. She struggled across, keenly aware that she couldn't use her arms for balance, as she fiercely held onto the cat. He was regaining a little strength and was beginning to squirm. She didn't have much time.

She reached the other side. The mother cat was sitting about five feet from the stream bank, watching Katie intently. A low growl emanated from deep inside her. Ignoring the sound, Katie gently set the cub down on the bank, then stepped back two strides. But then she stopped. She had just saved the lion's cub and she refused to retreat. She had a point to make. She wasn't even sure why she had to make the point, she just did. She had to show the big cat that she was no different from them, that they had nothing to fear from her.

The lion growled again, a little louder, but Katie refused to budge. The mother lifted her paw, showing her claws. Again, Katie didn't move. Finally, the lion focused her attention on her cub and ignored Katie completely.

Katie had made her point. She stepped back carefully until she reached the rock. She climbed onto it and just sat, watching the mountain lion. Every once in a while, as the mother was licking her cub, she would glance up at Katie.

"I'm not going anywhere," she said quietly, but loud enough to be heard by the lion. "In fact, let me introduce myself. Cat, my name is Katie." She stopped and thought. "No, my name is also Cat."

She knew from that moment, that she would never again be known as Katie. Her name was Cat ... with a C.

She made her way back to her horse, who had retreated into the woods, nervous to be in the vicinity of a mountain lion. She climbed onto Scooby's back and just sat there watching the two lions. The mother had the cub in her mouth and was carrying it back upstream. Just before Cat rode off, the mother stopped, set the cub down, and looked back at Cat. She stared for a full ten seconds, then picked up her cub again to make the journey back to her other cubs.

*****

Cat returned to her favorite flat rock by the stream the following week and the week after that. She spent as much time there as possible, often seeing the mother and cubs. They began to see her as a fixture of the scenery, never actually approaching her but knowing that, in fact, she was nothing to be feared.

More importantly, for Cat it was life-changing. She could live in the human community, interact with her fellow humans, but she knew that no matter what happened, her heart would always be in the animal kingdom.

Chapter 6

Three years later, the Pony Express came to town. We had often wondered just how many settlements existed out there. Enough time had passed for those who had spent the early years wandering to have finally settled down. We knew about Monett and Paradise, and word had filtered in over the years about others. Putney, Vermont was the furthest eastern settlement we had heard of, but we had also had new arrivals who spoke of communities in New York State, Kentucky, South Carolina, Iowa, and Michigan. But we knew there had to be others. The Pony Express riders answered that for us.

They arrived in Rock Creek on a rare day when both Ben and Lila were in town. They had taken Cat to the dentist and were on their way to have dinner with Sean and his family when the two riders came down the street. They each trailed a loaded pack mule.

The three waited for the riders to reach them. On one of the saddlebags were the words "Pony Express" in large letters crudely written in white paint.

The one closest reached out his hand to Ben. "I'm Steve.

This is Oliver. Can't believe we're finally here."

"Nice to meet you. I'm Ben, this is Lila, and our daughter Cat." He pointed to the sign. "This for real?"

"It is. It was about time the different settlements in the country communicated with each other, so Oliver and I took it upon ourselves to make it happen. 'Pony Express' seemed like an appropriate name. It was an important part of the settlement of the west. It can do the same thing now. Ben and Lila, huh? You the famous ones?"

"I guess."

"Lots of stories about you—even to this day. Most folks thought you died."

"We get that a lot. So what do you carry?"

"Letters, mostly. And lists of names of people at the various settlements. Over time, once we have accurate lists and we know who's still alive, it'll make our job easier. Right now we have to turn away lots of people who want us to bring messages to missing loved ones on the off-chance that they might be alive. If we did that for everyone, we'd need a dump truck to carry them all. So we're telling people to write letters to people that they know are in one of the other settlements. We don't have too many of those yet, but over time, once all the communities have resident lists from the others, we'll have more. Right now, our mission is to gather up names." He reached into the bag behind him and pulled out a letter. He handed it to Ben. "You've got mail. Huh, that phrase is a blast from the past. Anyway, a guy named Brian, the mayor of Monett, Missouri wanted to touch base with you. We were there a couple of months ago. Now that we know you are actually alive, we can give it to you."

Ben smiled and handed it to Lila. "Nice to know he's still the mayor."

"This is exciting," said Lila. "What a wonderful idea you came up with. It's a way to connect our country again."

"We're hoping we can inspire more people to help us," said Oliver. "Otherwise, the mail is going to be extremely slow. If we can establish a post office in each settlement and have enough people to work shorter routes, this could really work. A letter from Monett bound for Yellowstone could be delivered to Paradise, or to Deadwood, South Dakota, another small community. Once there, the person responsible for making the run to Yellowstone could take it. It might be a while before it's all in place, but once it is, a letter from, say, Vermont to Yellowstone might only take a month or two."

"So how many settlements are there?" asked Ben.

"We've been on the road for a little over two years. So far we've located twenty-seven. I'm sure there are more, but we feel we've done pretty well finding that many. This is as far west as we're going."

"How did you find all the towns?" asked Lila.

"Word of mouth. We didn't wander aimlessly, although we did find a few of them by accident. If we heard enough evidence that a community existed, then we'd try to find it."

"Do they vary much in size?" said Ben.

"They do. From what we hear, yours is the largest. The smallest has about twenty-five people. There are a few around that size. Most are in the 200 to 500 range. We've also been told of some communities in Canada, but we'll leave that to someone else. Just connecting the twenty-seven that we've found so far here in the States will be quite a chore."

"It's interesting," said Ben. "On one hand, knowing how devastating the event was, it's hard to imagine that many people surviving. On the other hand, When you think of how over-populated the country was and how few people there are now, it's mind boggling."

"We can easily go many days without seeing another person," said Oliver.

They reached Sean's house and introductions were made. Sean and Brittany immediately invited them to join the group for dinner.

"We also have a small guest house," said Sean. "You're welcome to stay there. I built it a few years ago just for times like these, when someone is passing through and needs a place to stay for a few days."

"Much obliged," said Steve. "It'll be nice to have a roof over our heads for a change."

The evening was spent discussing the other communities and getting Steve and Oliver's impressions of how people, in general, were adapting to the new world.

"For the most part, pretty well," Oliver expounded. "Some communities are more successful than others. I can tell already that yours is thriving. It has a good feeling to it. Monett, as well. Their population hovers close to 400, and it's well run. The place is clean and people seem happy. The other town I told you about, Deadwood, is doing well. They are not large—less than 200—but they are happy and the community is succeeding. The most successful ones are those in which the residents work together. Unfortunately, there are a few where egos take center stage and very little ever gets done. Paradise is one of those. I'm told the population has dropped from a high of about 500 a few years ago, to right around 150 now."

Ben was aware of that. Close to a hundred had migrated from Paradise to Yellowstone over the years, and he had heard the stories. Electricity or no electricity, Paradise didn't have the personalities to succeed.

"Why is this the furthest west you are going?" asked Brittany.

"First and foremost," answered Steve, "nobody has told us of any settlements west of here. They might exist, but we're not going to spend the next year wandering around looking for them. Also, south and west of here, it gets pretty mountainous. No thanks. We'll let someone else explore that area. As it is, we have our work cut out for us."

Ben brought up a few names of people they had met along the way, but Steve and Oliver hadn't run across them, the exception being Rob and Jenny, a couple headed for South Carolina with a daughter a little older than Cat. The two families had met when Ben and Lila were on their way to Yellowstone.

"Well, they made it to South Carolina," said Oliver. "They have one of the better settlements—around 250 people and thriving. Next time we're there, we will let them know you were asking about them."

"I'll write them a letter before you leave," said Lila.

"Now that we've visited all twenty-seven towns," said Steve, "we want to fine tune the organizing process. If you know of anyone who would like to be the official Pony Express person here, all they would have to do is visit Paradise and Deadwood once a month or so. Best to travel in pairs, just for safety against accidents."

"I'm sure we can find a couple of people," said Sean. "There is always someone looking for more to do."

A makeshift post office was set up in Sean's store and the lists of names of residents from the other settlements were copied by volunteers. The lists were kept in a binder for anyone to access. In some cases people recognized old acquaintances. But the problem most people had was that so many in the new world had stopped using their last names. So Joe Smith in Monett might have been any one of a half dozen Joes Ben and Lila had met who hadn't given their last names. It was all going to take time. But the enthusiasm for the idea was infectious.

When Steve and Oliver left a few days later, it was with over thirty letters. Many were bound for Paradise—former residents hoping to keep in touch with friends who had stayed—some were going to Monett, and a half dozen to various communities around the country.

*****

Over the next year, the Pony Express fell into place. Monthly runs were made between Yellowstone, Paradise, and Deadwood. From there, the mail was passed on from community to community. Steve and Oliver were right. Letters Lila sent to Jenny in South Carolina were answered and received only a couple of months later. It wasn't only letters that were exchanged, but life stories, as well. Pen pals were established and people made friends with others they would probably never meet in person. Recipes were passed on, as were community ideas that had been found successful. For the first time, people began to believe that there was a country again. It was fragmented, but it existed.

Reports from Paradise were encouraging as well. Because of the mail delivery, people were taking more of an interest in the town and a sense of community was finally being established. The bad apples had been weeded out and people with common sense and vision had taken over the town government.

All the while, the question was being asked in Yellowstone of what lay west of there. Could there, in fact, be other communities? One night, they were discussing it at a cookout Aaron and Emily were hosting.

"How far west have you been in your scavenging?" Ben asked Sean.

"Not far at all. As you know, I don't do much scavenging anymore, but when I did, I tended to go more south, toward Denver. So the furthest west I've been is maybe a hundred miles."

"I'd like to check it out sometime," said Aaron.

"Spoken like a man without children," said Sean. "It's harder for me to just head out like that. We could be gone months."

"Face it, you're a wimp."

"I could still beat the crap out of you."

"Oh God," said Emily. "Here they go again."

Their good-natured fighting had been a central part of their relationship from almost the day they met, so many years earlier in Marine boot camp.

Getting back on subject, Ben said, "We always heard that with the big earthquake they predicted would eventually hit California, half the state would slide into the sea. I think the quake they got after the event was even more massive than anything they could have predicted. I wonder if the coastline is closer to us now?"

Nick, who had been a meteorologist in St. Louis at the time of the event, turned to his partner Jason, who had been living in California. "You saw some of it."

"In my rearview mirror. I was driving that ancient pickup I'd found. How I made it to St. Louis is beyond me. It was a mess. I can almost guarantee that California fell into the ocean, but how far east of there is a question. Driving through parts of Arizona, Nevada, New Mexico, and whatever other states I hit, was murder. Fissures had cropped up everywhere. Sometimes I had to go hundreds of miles out of my way. I know it seems to be that way all over, but trust me, I'm talking whole sections of land—miles wide—just dropped away. What I'm getting at here is this: It's quite possible that some of these craters are linked, and if they are at all connected to the ocean and the ocean filled them up, it could seem as if the ocean had traveled that far eastward. That was the extreme southwest. And I will say that even with all that destruction, there were certain other areas in the southwest that didn't seem to be affected. So it's really impossible to predict. Who knows, this far north? We might be able to travel as far as Oregon, or we might encounter the ocean a couple hundred miles west of here. When Nick and I were doing all of our traveling, this was as far west as we got."

Upon further discussion, they all realized that no one living in Yellowstone, except Jason, had come from anywhere farther west.

"I think it's time somebody explored it," said Aaron.

Ben had to agree with him. He just wasn't sure he wanted

to be one of the explorers. He had done enough traveling and he was happy with his life. Why upset things?

A week later, the choice was taken out of his hands altogether.

Chapter 7

"She's gone." Ben and Lila's neighbor, Frank, had a look of panic on his face as he got off his horse.

"Who's gone?" asked Ben.

"Sophie. She took off with that asshole, Clete. It had to be his idea. He's bad news."

"Okay, try to calm yourself down. Tell me what happened."

Frank climbed down from his horse and took a breath.

"You know she's been hanging out with Clete, right?"

Ben nodded. He'd known this was coming. Sophie, once Cat's childhood friend, had become wild and uncontrollable in recent months. Only thirteen, she had "developed" earlier than most of the girls her age, and had no problem flaunting it. Despite having good parents, Sophie had been a problem for about a year. Two months earlier, she had started hanging around with Clete, a troubled boy three years older than herself. The Yellowstone board had actually had some serious discussions about Clete in recent months. He had been caught bullying younger boys and inappropriately spying on some of the girls.

Clete lived with an older couple who had found the

toddler a week after the event happened. He was dirty, hungry, and thirsty, so they took him with them as they wandered. They weren't particularly nice people, and they never struck Ben as the kind who would take on a young child. But he knew that some of the most hardened people had made allowances after the world collapsed.

They had shown up in Yellowstone a couple of years before Ben and Lila and pretty much kept to themselves. Clete had been given free reign from the moment they arrived, and had slowly built a reputation as someone the Yellowstone parents advised their kids to stay away from. That was enough incentive for Sophie to seek him out. To her, he was exciting. To him, Sophie was easy pickings. Rumor had it that their relationship had turned physical almost immediately, and there were many nights when Sophie didn't come home at all.

Lila had tried talking to Cat about it, but Cat, being a late bloomer, had trouble understanding the decisions Sophie had made—and understanding the relationship at all. She hadn't liked Sophie for quite a long time, and she instinctively stayed far away from Clete.

So, while Ben knew it was coming, it didn't relieve him of any responsibility. He knew he was going to have to help retrieve Sophie.

"She didn't come home again last night, so this morning I rode over to Clete's house and talked to the two clowns who call themselves his parents. I swear, I was about to punch them both out. They're fucking idiots who never should have been allowed to live here."

"Just tell me what happened."

"They left is what happened. The kids up and left.

Yesterday morning. They said they wanted to see the Pacific Ocean, so they packed a few things, stocked up on food and water, and took off. We've gotta get her back. She's given us some trouble, but she's still our daughter. Him, I'm going to kill."

"Frank, let's not get ahead of ourselves. One thing at a time. First, we find Sophie. I'll get the word out for volunteers. I'm sure she'll be fine. But I agree with you that we have to bring her back. She's too young to be traveling alone with someone like him. We can leave tomorrow morning."

"But we'll lose a whole day."

"You want me to snap my fingers and make a search party magically appear? People don't exactly live around the corner. It'll take all day to get the word out, then people have to pack and make arrangements. This could be a long trip. Go home and pack. We'll meet back here first thing in the morning."

Frank grudgingly left. He knew Ben was right, but he was understandably anxious to find his daughter. Ben felt for him. Frank had had so much trouble with Sophie, and at times had probably wished her gone. But now that she was gone, he'd give anything to get her back.

Word spread quickly. Although most felt the same reluctance as Ben to make the journey, considering the subjects involved, they also knew that a community sticks together, no matter what.

It was decided that the search party would consist of Ben, Aaron, Sean, Nick, and Jason, in addition to Frank. The five men had worked together many times and knew what to do. If they could, they would have preferred to have Frank stay home, but he would never allow that. As for the women, no one was being chauvinistic. Emily had a school to run, Lila had a town to run—not to mention watching over Cat—and Brittany had three children. Many more had volunteered, but Ben and the others felt that six would be enough.

They gathered at Ben and Lila's house early the next morning. They were pretty sure they'd be able to pick up the trail quickly. Despite growing up in Yellowstone, neither Clete nor Sophie was particularly savvy in the wilderness. They knew enough to get by, but that was all.

Ben said his goodbyes to his family, and they started on their way, hoping that they'd run across Clete and Sophie returning home, having realized that their journey was stupid. But they all knew they couldn't be so lucky. They just had to hope the two teens weren't already dead, having fallen into a hole or tripped down a cliff.

What to do with Clete and Sophie when they caught up with them was certainly the question of the day. Sophie would be dealt with by Frank, but Clete was another story. At sixteen, he was an adult in this new society. Going off with Sophie—no matter how wild she was herself—was tantamount to kidnapping. In the old world he would have been charged with rape, as well. The most they could do would be to banish him from the community, which they would certainly do. There was no place for him in Yellowstone.

As expected, picking up the teens' trail was simple. They had made no attempt to cover their tracks and were, in fact, quite sloppy. Broken branches and bits of food gave them a trail a child could follow.

They were on the western edge of Yellowstone now. It was an area that Ben had explored a couple of times before, but not enough to be familiar with it. Nick, Jason, and Sean, however, had all been that way many times. At three o'clock they ran across the remains of a campfire. They stopped for a quick rest.

"We're going faster than they are," said Aaron. "They wouldn't have stopped so early their first day. Means they're moving slowly. We still have three or four more hours of riding ahead of us. I predict we will find their second camp by noon tomorrow."

"We'll catch up to them the next day," said Frank, who had said relatively little the whole day. "And then I want Clete alone. You can all leave."

Ben turned to him. "I already made it clear about that. We're bringing them both back. If you can't live with that, turn around now."

"But he took my girl!"

"Your girl," said Nick, "went willingly. She's not innocent in all this. Clete will get what's coming to him. Your job will be to deal with Sophie. We'll take care of Clete."

Frank grudgingly nodded.

They found the next camp at two the following day, slightly later than Aaron's prediction, and the day after that they found the kids' campsite even later.

"They're speeding up," said Jason. "I wonder why."

"They've gotta know we're behind them," said Sean. "It started out as a lark, but now they realize that if they don't want to be caught, they'd better pick up the pace."

"Clete, in particular, must know that if they are caught, he's cooked," said Ben. "He's going to push Sophie along."

They stopped for the night on a high ridge, and Nick got out his map to try to determine where they were. It was now unfamiliar territory for them all. The terrain was beginning to change from mountainous to flat. More mountains were in the distance, but in between was prairie.

"So where are we?" asked Ben.

"Idaho," Nick answered, his finger on the map. He looked up to get his bearings, then down at the map again. He raised his head and pointed to the distant mountains. "That would be the home of some former national forests, like Sawtooth. If they've kept to the base of the mountain range, it should be easy going for them ... and for us."

"And if not?" asked Frank.

"Then they're stupid." He looked at Frank. "Sorry."

"You're just telling it like it is. The fact is, they are stupid."

Changing the subject, Nick said to them all, "What do you see? Or rather, what don't you see?"

Aaron won the prize. "Crevasses. Only a few of them."

"This is the west coast," said Jason. "Earthquake country. I know because I was running for my life down in California. We've all seen most of the country and how broken up it is. So why not here?"

"The crevasses are here," said Nick. "Just not as wide or as long. I don't have a definitive answer for you, but a guess would be that it has something to do with the rock formation underground. I think it's the reason we don't see a lot of it in Yellowstone. The underground rock might just be too solid here. Or it can shift as large plates, without breaking. That said, just because we don't see a lot of crevasses, it doesn't mean they aren't there. The prairie grass could have grown over some of the narrower ones, hiding them. So be careful."

The next few days were boring. The plains lacked the

beauty of the mountains, and all were wishing they were back home. But they had no trouble sticking to the kids' trail. It was obvious that they were getting tired and slowing down.

"What are they eating?" asked Sean. "They're obviously not hunting and we haven't passed too many places to fish."

"I had a lot of jerky," said Frank. "They cleaned me out."

"I'm sure that got old fast," said Ben. "At least there is plenty of water, so they're not going thirsty."

The trail took them into a town called Butte City. It was a tiny town of dilapidated houses, a bar, and a gas station.

"It says 'Population 68'," said Ben.

"Not anymore," replied Nick.

"They're getting desperate," said Aaron after they had looked around. "They tried breaking into some of these places. They're not going to find any food now."

"They also broke into the bar," said Jason. "I see a broken whiskey bottle. Recent."

"Great," said Frank. "Two stupid kids with alcohol. There's a good combination."

Ben had noticed that Frank was becoming more cynical as time went on. He was beginning to wonder if Frank even wanted to find Sophie. But of course he did. He was a father. But a father of what? A daughter who was just going to continue to disappoint him and his wife, Brenda? A daughter who was going to continue to make their life hell?

"Hey, they've changed direction," yelled Sean from the other side of town, not much more than fifty yards away. "They're heading into the hills."

"Like I said," said Frank, shaking his head. "Stupid."

"Any theories on why they would change direction?" asked

Ben. "Going into the hills means they're no longer shooting for the Pacific."

"I think I might have found a clue," said Aaron. "I don't think Sophie is a willing participant any longer."

They gathered around, not far from the front door of the bar.

"Look at the ground."

The signs were obvious. Instead of two sets of clear footprints in the dust, the ground was disturbed. Something had gone on.

"A fight," said Aaron. Sean had come over to see what was happening. Aaron continued, "You can see lots of footprints—the same two people, not any additional footprints—but there," he pointed, and then pointed to three other spots, "and there, and there, and there. Bodies hit the ground."

"Couldn't they have just gotten drunk and ... and ..." Frank was having trouble getting the words out.

"And had wild sex?" finished Nick.

Frank nodded dumbly.

"In the middle of the dust?" asked Ben. "I would doubt it."

"Definitely a fight," said Aaron, "ending with someone getting hurt." He knelt over a broken whiskey bottle. "There's a little blood on the bottle and another few drops on the ground."

"And drag marks," added Sean. "Those are heel marks. They lead away about thirty feet, then disappear, right where hoofprints begin. Someone was dragged over to the horses and put on one of the horses."

"Can you tell who?" asked Frank. It was clear to Ben that Frank wasn't thinking rationally, or he wouldn't have asked the question.

"Clete is sixteen and has about a hundred pounds on thirteen year old Sophie," said Sean. "You do the math."

Ben could see that everyone was getting a little testy, and it was easy to know why. This was more than they had signed up for. They all thought it would be a simple case of catching two wayward teens, showing them the error of their ways, and bringing them back home. Well, nobody thought it would be *that* simple, but they certainly didn't expect this.

"What do you think happened?" asked Frank, not really wanting to hear the answer.

"I think Sophie had finally had enough," answered Aaron. "I think she was tired and hungry and had finally figured out that Clete was the asshole everyone had told her he was. There was no way Clete could come back, so a fight ensued. He changed direction because it's easier to get lost in the hills."

"It's taken on a new dimension," said Ben. "I suggest we get moving."

Ten minutes later, they were heading into the hills, hoping for the best, but each one secretly expecting the worst.

Those fears were realized a couple of hours later, when they were riding along a trail that took them near the edge of a cliff.

Jason, who had taken the lead, suddenly let out an "Oh my God!" and jumped off his horse. The others followed and they all peered over the side of the cliff. Fifty feet below them on a flat rock lay the lifeless body of Sophie.

Chapter 8

It was so exciting! She was finally getting away from her overbearing and demanding parents. Complete assholes, both of them. They gave her such a hard time about her relationship with Clete. She was old enough. She was thirteen. Her parents were always talking about how much things had changed in this new world, how in the old days girls weren't ready for a relationship until they were sixteen or seventeen. Well, first of all, she never knew the "old" world, and second, that was bullshit anyway. They talked about these things in school, and she had read enough books to know that even in the "old" world, girls were having sex at thirteen. Her parents were just trying to scare her.

And she wasn't stupid. She knew that Clete was trouble. She'd have to be a complete idiot not to see that. He was big for his age and looked to be nineteen or twenty, and he had a bad reputation. But he was fun and he was dangerous, and she liked that. Let's face it, she often thought, the world her parents used to know was filled with excitement and danger. Here, other than coming up on a mother bear and her cub and having to run for your life, there was nothing—no excitement at all.

Everything had to do with surviving. Well, she was done with that. She had survived. Now it was time to have some fun.

Clete was the one who had suggested the trip. No one in Yellowstone had seen the Pacific Ocean—at least, no one had seen it since before the big event. They could write down what they found and come back with the information. Maybe then they wouldn't be seen as losers. Or maybe they would like what they found and decide to live there. That was Clete's suggestion, but as exciting as he was, Sophie couldn't actually see living with him without anyone else around. It would get boring fast. But they could cross that bridge when they got to it.

Clete said they needed to bring food, but didn't have a lot of room for it. Sophie knew her dad kept a large box of homemade jerky, and had stolen it the day before when her parents were in town. They stuffed their saddlebags with it and filled two canteens each with water. They took along some extra clothes, plus a jacket and a rain poncho each.

They left early in the morning, before Clete's parents were up, and headed west. Clete had a map and had worked out the best route, along the prairie at the edge of some hills. He told her it would be an easy ride, and if a lot of the west coast had, in fact, fallen into the ocean, they might be a lot closer to the ocean than they thought.

The first day was pretty, riding through quiet forests, and stopping twice to have sex on the forest floor. Neither one of them had ever done anything this daring, and just the thought of what they were doing made them horny.

But as early as the second day, Sophie began to see a slight change in Clete. He was looking over his shoulder a lot and insisting that they ride a little faster. There was no sex in the woods that day.

"What's wrong?" Sophie finally asked.

"Your dad and the others are going to come after us, and if they catch us, I'm a dead man."

"Why?"

"Why? I'm sixteen and I'm taking a girl away from her parents."

"I'm not a girl."

"You're fucking thirteen. To them, you're a girl."

"Why don't we just go back and say we were out for the day and got lost?" All of a sudden, the trip had lost some of its excitement.

"They'd never believe that. No, they'd shoot me or kick me out, or something. Our best bet is to find the Pacific and come back heroes.

Sophie wasn't totally sure Clete believed that himself, but it was the rationale they used. From then on, looking over their shoulders at the trail behind them became the norm.

By the time they reached the prairie, Sophie was ready to go back, and said as much to Clete.

"Fine. Go back. You'll get lost and die in the woods somewhere, but if that's what you want, go ahead."

"Can't you come back with me?"

"I already explained. I can't."

"But I don't want to go back alone."

"Stay with me or go back alone. They're your only choices."

"This isn't fun anymore. I want to go home."

Clete didn't respond. He just kept riding.

The turning point came when they reached Butte City. It was an ugly little town, thought Sophie. Was it even a town at all? The sign said sixty-eight people lived there before the event. Could sixty-eight even be called a town? She thought they were all a lot bigger back then.

Sophie desperately wanted to go home. Clete had become sullen and sometimes even mean. Going with him had been a big mistake. She was trying to decide if she could find her way home, when she heard Clete let out a whoop of joy from a building that had a faded "Bar" sign out front. That couldn't be good. Clete had told her to break into some of the houses—broken down shacks would be more like it—and she if she could find any cans of food. That showed her just how desperate Clete was. There was no way Sophie would eat anything in a can so many years after everyone died. There wouldn't be anything good at this point.

But the fact was, they were hungry. They only had a little jerky left, and they were sick of it. Neither one of them was much of a hunter. Clete had tried killing some rabbits the day before, but missed each time. So many of the kids at Yellowstone were good hunters. Sophie wasn't, but had never cared—her father had done the hunting for the family. And now she had picked someone as useless as herself to travel with.

Clete came out of the door to the bar waving a smallish, already half-empty bottle of something. He danced a jig in the dirt and almost fell over.

"Look what I found," he said, slurring his words.

Sophie had seen her parents get drunk a couple of times, and it had taken them a lot longer than that. She had heard her mother talk about people who couldn't hold their alcohol. Now she knew what her mother meant. Clete was already feeling the effects. She also thought he might be exaggerating just a little bit.

"Sophie, come and get some. Someone already raided it, but there are still a few bottles left. Let's get drunk."

"Clete," Sophie said hesitantly as she approached him. "I don't think it's a good idea."

"You afraid?" Clete gave her a nasty look. "I knew I should have done this trip with a real woman, not a little girl."

"I'm not a little girl! I just don't think you should be drinking. You're already drunk."

"And I'm not stopping here." He threw away the bottle and went back into the bar. When he came out, he had a large bottle of bourbon. He couldn't open it, so he took one of his heavier knives and swung it against the bottle, breaking the top off. He took a swig, keeping the jagged, broken edge, away from his mouth. He made a face as he swallowed it and Sophie realized that Clete didn't actually like the taste. He just wanted to get drunk.

Well, screw him. She wasn't going to stand around and watch him drink. She left him standing in the dust outside the bar and went to one of the houses to see if there was anything she needed. Food wouldn't be an option, but maybe there would be something else—anything to keep her occupied and away from Clete.

She managed to spend an hour in the house, looking at all the things her parents used to talk about—a TV, a refrigerator, some black box on the kitchen counter that she couldn't remember the name of, and many other things. It was fascinating, but all the while she could hear Clete calling out her name to come and party with him. He really was drunk now—there was no need to exaggerate.

The sun started to go down and she knew it was time to leave. She stopped at the front door and looked over at Clete. He was quiet now, urinating against the wall of the bar. What could she have ever seen in him? He zipped up, turned, and saw her standing there. He raised his bottle with the jagged top—she wasn't sure if it was the same one from before or a new one—and silently saluted her, then leaned back against the wall.

She walked across what was probably once a road and approached him with her hand out.

"Why don't you give me the bottle."

"You want some?"

"No, I just think..."

"Then shut the fuck up."

"Clete, you've had enough."

"I'll tell you when I've had enough. You've been nothing but trouble this whole trip with your whining. Why'd I let you come with me?"

He was slurring badly and Sophie was having trouble understanding him.

Clete closed his eyes for a moment and Sophie reached for the bottle. He must have felt her presence, because his eyes shot open and he jerked the bottle up and away, raking Sophie's palm and fingers with the sharp edge. She cried out in pain. With blood dripping, she cradled her hand in her t-shirt.

"Why did you do that?"

"You bitch. You tried to take it from me. Get your own."

"I'm bleeding!"

"Not my problem."

"Clete, stop it. You're drunk and you're getting really mean." Her hand was bleeding profusely. She turned and walked to her horse to get a towel from her saddlebags.

"Where are you going?" He pushed himself away from the wall and charged her.

"I'm just getting..." She turned just as he reached her, and she saw the bottle coming at her head.

She never felt the blow that killed her.

Clete dropped the bottle and stood over Sophie, splayed out on the ground, unmoving.

"You're not going to leave me, you bitch."

And then a change came over him.

"Sophie? Are you okay? I'm sorry I hit you so hard. Are you okay? Sophie?"

He fell to his knees and shook her. "Sophie, wake up. I'm sorry."

He was crying now. He laid down next to her with his arm draped over her lifeless body, and then he fell into a drunken sleep.

*****

He awoke with his arm still on Sophie. The sun was bright, and he was squinting. His head was pounding and his mouth was dry ... so dry. He was disoriented. He looked over at Sophie.

"Wake up. We've gotta go."

He raised up to an elbow and shook Sophie.

"Hey, wake ..." And then he remembered. It came back to him in a rush. He pulled his hand back quickly and stared at

Sophie.

"Sophie?" The tears came again. "Noooo! What did I do? Sophie, please wake up. I'm sorry. I didn't mean it."

He knew she wasn't getting up. He got to his feet and stared down at her lifeless body. Self-preservation mode kicked in. He couldn't leave her there for any of the Yellowstone crowd to find. He had to hide the body. Should he bury her? He could, but what would his story be if they caught up with him? Maybe she turned around and went back on her own. He had no idea what happened to her after that. Too flimsy. He'd still get blamed. Somehow, he was going to be blamed no matter what, so he'd make her death an accident. He could play up the angle that they were very much in love. She fell off a cliff and he was devastated by her death. That was flimsy too, but better than the other explanation. What it boiled down to was that he was just going to have to disappear. Maybe he could find another settlement to live in.

First things first. He had to get rid of the body. Any sentimental feelings he once had for Sophie were gone. Now he had a job to do. He brought her horse over, then picked up Sophie. She was a lot heavier than he expected, and she was stiff. Not too stiff, but not flexible either. He remembered having to bury a guy who had died. It was hot, like it was here. Rigor had set in a couple of hours after he died, and then his body became flexible again after about twelve hours. That was probably the case with Sophie. She would loosen up as they rode.

It was a struggle, but he got her draped over the saddle. He found some thin rope and tied her hands and feet to the cinch rings on either side of the horse. The smell of death made the horse skittish, complicating Clete's efforts. Once she was finally secure, he got on his own horse, grabbed the reins of the other, and started up into the hills.

A couple of hours into the ride, he found the perfect spot, a steep cliff on the side of the trail. With little sentimentality, he untied Sophie, pulled her off the horse, and dragged her over to the cliff. With an insincere "Bye, Sophie," he rolled her off the edge. He purposely didn't watch her body fall, but he heard the sickening thud as she hit bottom.

Clete grabbed one of the last pieces of jerky from Sophie's horse's saddlebag, mounted his horse, grabbed her horse's reins, and started up the trail. First order of business; he had to find something other than jerky to eat.

Three hours into his journey he was looking for a place to rest when something hit him hard in the lower back. The force was so strong, he fell off his horse. It wasn't until he hit the ground that the pain from the blow set in. It was excruciating. He had never felt anything like it. He reached around and felt it. An arrow! There was blood everywhere. He passed out.

*****

Someone was slapping him across the face.

"Wake up."

He opened his eyes to find a shaggy man looking back at him. The man had a full beard and hair past his shoulders. He wasn't young, There was a lot of gray in the hair. When he opened his mouth, Clete saw that he had only half his teeth, and he had a body odor worse than anything Clete had ever smelled. The man looked away.

"He's awake." He was talking to others. And that's when Clete noticed them, at least a dozen other men peering at him each just as shaggy in his own way as the first one.

The pain in his back was unbearable. But he was lying on his back now, so the arrow must've been taken out. There was another pain, equally as excruciating. His hand. He tried to turn his head to look at what was causing the pain, and that's when he noticed it. He was tied to something. He turned his head right and then left. Stakes. He was tied to stakes. And, he suddenly realized, he was completely naked. He focused in on the pain now. He was missing a finger! He could see it in the dirt next to his hand. There was a puddle of blood on the ground, but the finger had clotted. He cried out in pain and fear.

The man who was standing over him said, "We know you are human, so that means you were trespassing. This is our land."

Clete was sobbing now. "I didn't mean to." His throat was very dry and he had trouble getting the words out. "I'll leave."

"Too late for that. Shoulda thought of it before you trespassed."

"What are you going to do?" Clete said, his voice choking.

"I guess we have to leave a warning for anyone else who thinks they're going to pass through our land. They see you and they'll turn back, for sure.

Six of the men gathered around him, all brandishing long hunting knives.

And then Clete screamed.

Chapter 9

Frank knelt down by the cliff face, his whole body heaving as he tried to catch his breath. No words would come. Finally, a long, low wail erupted from deep within him. Hard to hear at first, it got steadily louder, until it became a mournful cry of anguish. This continued for several minutes until Ben knelt down next to him and put his arm around the man's back. Frank turned around and put his arms around Ben, shaking as he cried. Finally, Ben heard the choked words, "My baby." Frank let go of Ben and collapsed onto the ground.

Ben said to the others, "He fainted."

"It was too much for him," said Jason. "His body just shut down. It was the only way to deal with it."

"I think I see a way down," said Sean. "Over there is a rock fall."

"I'll go with you," said Ben.

The others left an unconscious Frank, after moving him into shade away from the cliff, and scouted the area for signs of Clete, while Ben and Sean worked their way over the tumbled rocks to get to Sophie—a task that had seemed easier from a distance. After a few slips and numerous bruises, the two men made it to the bottom, faced with the gruesome task of dealing with the body of Sophie. She was most definitely dead, her head turned at an unnatural angle.

"Think she slipped and fell?" asked Ben.

"Do you?"

"No. I was just hoping it was something simple like that."

As hard as it was, Sean was attempting to examine Sophie.

"Not much blood for such a long fall," he said. "Almost none. And look at this."

Even with all the death Ben had seen over the years, it was hard for him to look, but he forced himself. They were going to have to carry the body up the slope, so he was eventually going to have to get up close and personal.

"Look at the bruise on the side of her head."

"From the fall?"

"I don't think so," said Sean. "When she fell, she landed on the right side of her head." He grimaced as he lifted her head slightly off the ground. "Although you'd think there'd be a lot of blood…"

"Unless she was already dead?"

"Yeah. Dead bodies don't bleed. The bruise on her left temple is ugly and it's pretty fresh. But I think it happened before the fall."

"So she was dead and Clete threw her over?"

"That would be my assumption. Of course, we haven't located Clete yet."

They started the gruesome task of carrying Sophie's body up the dangerous slope. They made it up with only a few more bruises, then set Sophie down on one half of a blanket Aaron had laid out. They draped the other half of the blanket over

Sophie. Just in time, as Frank was now sitting up and looking over at them.

"I want to see her," he said in a soft voice.

"Do you think that's a good idea?" asked Ben.

"I want to see her."

He stood up and shakily made his way over to the blankets. He sat down next to the body and lifted up a corner of the blanket. The tears came again in a rush and he began sobbing again, this time quietly. The other men gave him his space. Nick motioned for Ben to join him up the trail.

"We found Clete's trail," he said. "He continued on in the same direction. I don't know where he's headed—frankly, I doubt he does either. At this point he is probably just wanting to get as far away as possible."

"We'll leave as soon as we bury Sophie," said Ben.

"Frank won't be happy with burying Sophie way out in the middle of nowhere," said Nick.

He wasn't. When he had regained his composure, Ben suggested that they find a spot to bury Sophie near there.

"No. I'm taking her back to Yellowstone. I'm taking her home."

"Frank, I don't want to get too graphic here," said Aaron, "but you're dealing with a decomposing body. Yellowstone is many days' ride from here, in the heat..." He left the rest unsaid.

"I'm not leaving my daughter out here in the middle of nowhere. She deserves to be home." More tears rolled down his cheeks. "I don't care about Clete anymore. I know he killed my daughter, but I can't do it any longer. I don't have it in me. If you want to go after him, you can. I just want to get my Sophie home. I'm taking her home."

The other men looked at each other. They knew they had to keep going, at least a little bit longer.

"Okay," said Sean. "We won't stop you, but here's what I suggest: stop in Butte City and search the houses and that bar for a plastic tarp. Cover her with it, find some rope, and tie the tarp as tightly as possible. Even that's not going to be enough—you remember what people looked like after the event, right? I'm just being realistic here. Find a shovel and take it with you. You might have to bury her somewhere along the way, but if you do, at least it will be closer to home."

Frank nodded absently and bent down to gently pick up his daughter. The others helped Frank secure Sophie's body on the back of his horse. When he was in the saddle, he looked down at his friends. For a moment he couldn't say anything.

"Thank you," he finally said. "Thank you for understanding my need to go home. You are the best friends a person could have. Hopefully I can repay you someday." He faltered, then turned his horse. "I have to go."

They watched him ride off, a man who survived the greatest catastrophe in human history and the difficult years that followed; a man who raised a daughter under the most difficult of circumstances and saw her take a road that all parents in the history of the world have always feared for their children. And now he was going home a broken man, broken not by the world events, but by a wayward daughter and a misguided young man. The world was cruel.

"How long do we follow him?" asked Ben.

"I say we give it a day," said Sean. "He's stupid and he has no wilderness skills. He'll die."

"And if we do catch him?" asked Jason.

Quiet.

"I guess we deal with it when the time comes," Aaron finally said.

*****

As it turned out, they didn't need the whole day. A couple of hours later they rounded a bend and stopped suddenly. Nick jumped off his horse and threw up in the brush by the side of the trail. Jason got off his horse and joined his partner, rubbing Nick's back. Ben, Aaron, and Sean pulled out their rifles and got off their horses, looking to the rocks and hills around them. Finally determining that they were alone, they lowered their guns and focused on the scene before them.

"Holy shit," said Aaron.

Nick and Jason joined them, Nick wiping his mouth.

"Sorry," he said. "With everything we've witnessed over the years, I thought I was immune to scenes like this."

They had found Clete, or what was left of him. He was lying on his back in the middle of the trail. He was completely naked, covered by ants and bugs feeding on his blood. His limbs had been cut off and piled next to his body. Most of his organs had been removed. There was very little left of what had once been Clete.

Written in blood on his chest were the words *Our land.*

"I guess this answers the question of whether or not there is anyone west of Yellowstone," said Ben, his mouth suddenly dry.

"Who would do this?" asked Nick.

"People we don't want to mess with," said Sean. "I say it's time to turn back. No sense in fighting a battle we don't need to fight."

"I guess burying Clete is out of the question," said Jason.

"You want to do it?" asked Aaron.

"Hell, no. He got what he deserved. And frankly, I'm more than a little spooked."

While they talked, Sean examined the body more carefully. Ben stayed on guard, looking into the hills around them. He suddenly saw a flash of light from high up in the rocks. Sun reflecting off a gun barrel? There was movement off to the left. A face was peering over a rock, studying them. It was an older man with long dirty hair. The man's face had the leathery look that reminded Ben of his horse's saddle—a face that had spent many years exposed to the sun. He didn't seem to care that Ben saw him. In fact, Ben wondered if that was the purpose.

"Time to go," he said urgently. "They're out there watching us."

They quickly mounted up and headed back down the trail, looking over their shoulders as they rode. Ben turned back for a moment and raised his hand in the direction of the man he saw, hoping they'd get the message: *We're gone and we're not going to bother you.*

*****

They rode in silence, each man deep in his own thoughts. None of them had seen anything so chilling in a long time.

"I saw one of them," Ben finally said. "He was older, but had a wild look to him. He's been out here a long time." He described more fully what he'd seen of the man.

"These people, and there were a number of them based on the foot prints—barefoot prints, I might add—almost seemed to enjoy what they were doing," said Sean. "And based on Clete's expression, he was awake for some of it." He let that sink in before he continued. "We've all seen a lot of different types of people and groups in our travels, but I don't think we've encountered anyone like these people. Based on what we saw of Clete's body and Ben's description of the guy he saw, I think we're dealing with a group that took a whole different direction—a step backward, so to speak. They went primitive. They probably have very little memory of who they might have once been."

"A group to steer clear of, for sure," said Aaron.

"Do you think they pose a threat to Yellowstone?" asked Jason.

"I doubt it," said Sean. "We're far enough away that I doubt they even know our community exists. And by saying 'Our land', they are probably very territorial."

They lapsed back into silence, all looking over their shoulders on a regular basis until they felt they were far enough away.

*****

When they reached Butte City, they encountered yet another blow in a very sad trip. Frank's horse was tied in front of one of the houses. Frank was nowhere to be seen.

"Did he take our advice and decide to bury Sophie here?" asked Jason.

"Frank?" called out Aaron.

No reply.

Ben's stomach turned. He had a bad feeling.

Behind the house was a grove of trees. Footprints in the dust indicated that Frank had headed in that direction. They approached the trees slowly. It was deadly quiet. Aaron and Sean pulled out their guns and looked around.

When the group reached the trees, they stopped and stared.

"Oh God," said Ben quietly.

Frank was leaning up against a rock with his arm around Sophie. A pistol was lying in the dirt next to Frank, and blood was all over the rock and the ground behind him. He had shot himself. In his lap, speckled with blood, was a piece of paper with the words: *I can't do it anymore.*

*****

I somehow thought that anyone who had lived this long after the catastrophe of so long ago had learned to accept the world they now lived in. Not everyone had totally embraced it, but I assumed they had accepted it. Maybe the only thing keeping Frank going was the responsibility of being a parent. With Sophie gone, maybe he realized that there was nothing left for him. He was just tired and it was time to end it. How many others were in the same position? Could it be that there were a lot more than I imagined? Had people not embraced the new world as much as I thought they had?

They buried Frank and Sophie together, the way Frank

would have wanted it. When they were done, they stood over the grave and said a few words. Frank and Sophie were far from home, but did it really matter? It was just their bodies. Ben hoped that if an afterlife did exist, they had found something better. Their pain was gone now. Telling Brenda that her husband and daughter were dead was going to be the final step in this long and brutal trip.

The burial done, the men got on their horses and began the long journey back home.

Chapter 10

The year Cat turned fourteen she met Simon. Yellowstone had seen very little growth from outside sources for a number of years. The largest influx had been from the ex-Paradise residents a few years before. It was assumed that by this time most people had stopped wandering and had finally settled down in one of the couple dozen communities across the country. The occasional family or lone straggler still showed up from time to time, usually from one of the Midwestern towns, tired of the endless plains and harsh winters, and succumbing to the lure of the mountains.

Simon's family was different. They had made the long trek from an Upstate New York community to Yellowstone because they needed "a change." They never offered up more information than that. However, the board liked them instantly and approved their relocation to Yellowstone. They found a secluded plot of land a couple of miles from Ben and Lila and, as was the tradition, had their house built in a couple of weeks with the help of many neighbors. Being summer, school wasn't in session, so little was seen of Simon.

All Cat knew of Simon, from having met him twice, both

times briefly, was that he was her age—a child of the new world—and seemed nice, but shy. He was also scrawny for his age, which was unusual. Most children had developed strong bodies early in life from all of the time spent outdoors. Cat was surprised at the lack of muscles in his upper body. It looked as if he had done very little labor in his life. His parents, on the other hand, looked like they belonged in the world. Simon's father, Mike, was a massive man—6'4" and at least 250 pounds, most of it muscle. Simon's mother, Linnea, a tall attractive woman a few years older than Cat's parents, was also muscular and capable. Both of Simon's parents seemed kind and were working hard to fit into the Yellowstone way of life, but, while friendly, were also overly mindful of their privacy. Cat's parents planned to have them over for a day, but one thing or another always seemed to get in the way of their plans. As a result, Cat still knew little about them.

Not that they were ignored. Nick and Jason in particular—loners themselves—felt a kinship with the new family and spent a lot of time helping them get settled. Cat figured she could wait until school started to get to know Simon.

*****

It was a beautiful summer day, warm but with a breeze that cooled the air considerably. Cat was riding Scooby along a trail she had found the summer before. She assumed it was an old animal trail, but one still used regularly, judging by the scat. It meandered through a forest, across a barren hilltop, and down into a narrow gorge. She loved the gorge for its rock formations and craters. She often wondered if it had been volcanic at some point in the distant past.

Like everyone else, she was well-armed whenever she went out. A .44 caliber lever-action Winchester rode beside her in its scabbard, and a 9 mm revolver hugged her hip. While her parents preferred semi-automatics, Cat liked the simplicity and feel of the revolver.

Despite her almost lifelong skill with guns, she rarely used them. She carried them for protection only. When she hunted, she used her crossbow—now a full-sized model—because she hated the sound of the guns and how they disturbed her connection with nature.

But today wasn't a hunting trip. Today was a thinking trip. She had been having feelings of late that she wasn't used to. Feelings of desire. She had had enough discussions with her mom to understand the feelings from a mental standpoint, but understanding them and actually feeling them were very different. She remembered Sophie and her relationship with Clete just a year earlier. At the time she could only understand it intellectually. Now it had a new meaning.

There were some boys in the community she was attracted to physically. The problem was, there was nothing else about them she wanted anything to do with. Yes, they were friends. One couldn't help but to be friends with practically everyone in a settlement this small, but they all had different outlooks than she did. They didn't feel the same kinship with nature. They lived in nature every day, but somehow had never learned to embrace the deeper parts of their relationship with it.

Many of the girls her age and even younger already had boyfriends, but not Cat. It made her sad to some extent, but at the same time she didn't know where a boyfriend could possibly fit into her life. There was one boy, Zack, who was three years older than Cat and had shown a lot of interest in her. He was nice enough, and certainly handsome—already almost the size of her dad and pretty capable—but just not someone she wanted to spend time with. She would much rather ride out alone, as she was doing today, than to spend time with Zack doing ... well, she wasn't exactly sure what.

She skirted a large rock that had been violently pulled from the ground—probably in the earthquake that Nick and Jason had often told her about that had happened in the west about a year before she was born. The east coast earthquake—the third of the massive quakes to hit the country—had occurred when she was just a few months old. Her parents had told her many stories about what they were doing in that earthquake. They had been apart and had seen it in different places and from different viewpoints.

But both quakes had completely changed the landscape of the country, forming craters and creating mountains where there weren't any before. She had trouble picturing what the country had looked like before. She saw the pictures in books, but it didn't help. That world seemed unreal and ugly. She couldn't imagine anything as beautiful as what she saw every day.

As she rounded the enormous boulder she saw a horse at the base of a cliff—a saddled horse. It was a mixture of light and dark gray, with some white on its nose. She knew many of the horses owned by the Yellowstone people, and this one didn't look familiar. She stopped and surveyed the scene. These were the times she missed Ralph. Her best friend and companion all her life had died earlier that year. He was old and hadn't traveled with her in a couple of years, but she remembered his younger days when the two of them would explore the countryside together. If any danger was close by, Ralph would be the first to notice it and would warn her. She had cried when he died—one of the few times in her life she had cried.

But he wasn't here now, so it was up to her to scope out the potential danger. She pulled out her rifle and laid it across her saddle. Better safe than sorry. She approached the horse slowly, looking in all directions as she went. When she got close, she dismounted and walked up to the horse. It had a cut on its left flank. Nothing serious, but the nature of the cut told her that the horse had fallen recently. She saw scratches on the glass-like rock caused by the horse's hooves. It fell here, on the smooth surface.

The horse was standing near a crevasse—more like a hole than a crevasse, as it only extended twenty feet in any direction. She looked over the edge. Sitting on the floor of the hole, fifteen feet below, was Simon, gingerly holding his left arm to his body. His faced was masked in pain. Sweat was dripping down his face and had soaked his shirt. He looked up to see Cat peering over the side.

"Hey," he said feebly. "I think I might need some help."

"Hi Simon. Are you okay? I don't know if you remember me, but I'm Cat."

"I do. I'm glad you showed up. I think my arm might be broken."

"What happened?"

"My horse slipped and went down, throwing me into this

hole. There are a few handholds, but because of my arm, I can't do anything about them. I'm stuck down here."

"I'll throw you down a rope and tie it to my horse. He can pull you up."

"I won't be able to tie it around me. My arm is in bad shape."

"I'll come down." Cat went back to Scooby, put the rifle back in its scabbard and unfastened her rope from the saddle. She didn't want to tie it to Scooby until she could guide the horse while he pulled Simon up, so instead, she tied it securely to a rock and threw the free end down into the hole. Holding onto the rope, she walked down the side of the hole with ease, ending up next to Simon.

"You did that so easily," he said in awe. Cat could hear the pain in the quaver of his voice.

"Your arm really hurts." She said it more as a statement than a question.

"Excruciating."

"How long have you been here?" As she talked, she wrapped the rope around his middle and tied it in a secure knot.

"I don't know. Three or four hours, I guess. If it wasn't for my arm, I wouldn't have minded it so much. Kind of peaceful."

Cat smiled to herself. It was something she might have said herself.

She heard a rumble and looked up. The sky had turned black. In the gloom of the hole, she didn't notice the clouds come in. Another rumble, closer this time. Now she saw lightning. She counted. She only got to two when the thunder crashed above them.

And then the rain came in sheets, soaking them in seconds.

Simon looked scared, but he tried to maintain a confident air.

"If it rains hard enough," he joked, "We can float to the top of the hole."

With the next flash of lightning and the immediate thunder, Cat was suddenly terrified.

"We have to get out of here fast!"

"I was kidding about the rain filling the hole."

"You don't understand," said Cat. "This hole *will* fill up, and if we don't get out of here, we're both going to drown."

Simon gave her a puzzled look.

"We might only have minutes. A flash flood is going to come down this gorge. And when it does, we won't stand a chance!"

Chapter 11

A look of comprehension came to Simon's face.

"You go up first," he said, "and tie it to your horse."

"If my horse is still there and hasn't been scared off by the lightning." She scrambled up the rope as easily as she had come down. When she got to the top, as she suspected, the two horses were nowhere to be seen. Scooby was loyal, but Cat knew that even the most loyal of horses could scare in a storm of this intensity.

The rain was coming down so hard now she was having trouble seeing the edge of the hole. How quickly the weather had turned. But she was used to it. Her mom and dad had told her that when the event happened almost a year before she was born, it changed all the weather patterns. Ever since then, violent storms were commonplace.

She yelled down to Simon, barely hearing her own voice in the downpour. "I'm going to pull you up. Try to step in the notches on your way up. It will help relieve some of the weight."

Simon nodded and grabbed hold of the rope with his good arm. As Cat pulled, Simon tried to use the uneven cliff face to work his way up. Despite Simon's light body weight and his use of the notches, he was still heavy for Cat. The rain made it particularly difficult. He made it halfway, then slipped on a notch and fell to the ground, the sudden shift in weight being too much for Cat. She fell down, losing hold of the rope. She heard Simon let out a cry from below.

Cat yelled down to him. "Are you okay?"

"I'll live."

"Then let's try it again."

Simon struggled to his feet and grabbed hold of the rope again, pulling it close to his body. Cat held on with all her might, trying desperately to avoid being pulled into the hole. It took a few tense minutes, but finally, Simon's good arm appeared over the lip and he pulled himself up. Cat abandoned the rope and grabbed Simon by the collar to help him up over the edge. They collapsed in a heap, trying to catch their breath.

However, the rest was short-lived. Already, water was rushing down the gorge. Six inches deep at the moment, Cat knew it would only be a matter of minutes before they faced the full force of the flood. The horses were nowhere to be seen and Cat could only hope that Scooby had made it back into the forest, well above the gorge.

Unfortunately, she and Simon would never reach the forest in time. With the speed the gorge was filling with water, the forest was too far away to attempt escape in that direction. Their only hope was the rocky cliff next to the hole. If there were enough handholds and cracks, they could make it safely above the rushing water. Cat wasn't sure how high they'd have to climb, not knowing how high the water would get, but they had to try. Simon's broken arm was going to give them a problem, but they had no choice.

"Simon," she yelled. "We have to get up this cliff. Do you think you can do it?"

"I'll do it."

"Then let's go."

Already, the powerfully rushing water was knee deep. It was hard for them to keep their balance. They reached the side of the cliff and Cat searched for a way up. Nothing jumped out at her. The rock wall was smoother than it first appeared. She climbed onto a boulder and frantically looked for something—anything—that would get them above the rapidly rising flood waters. She looked down at Simon. The water was to his waist. He was white as a ghost and looked to be ready to pass out from the pain of the broken arm.

"Grab my hand," she yelled. She knelt down on the boulder and reached out to him. He nodded absently and grabbed her hand. His broken arm now dangled helplessly by his side. Cat pulled and Simon used a smaller rock to help him onto the boulder. For a moment they were safe, but Cat knew it wouldn't last. She didn't know how deep the water would get, but knew they weren't high enough. She looked up and immediately saw what she was searching for—a ledge!

It was about twenty feet up. It would be high enough, but getting there would be a problem. Or not. Deep within the recesses of the cliff, she saw the way up. It was in the shadows, which is why she hadn't seen it before. It was a natural staircase that led to the ledge. It would still require much care, but if they took it slowly, they might just make it before the water—which was already to the top of the boulder—overtook them.

"Take my hand and follow me," she said to Simon. She could see that he was in serious danger of passing out. She just needed him to stay awake long enough to make it to the ledge. There was no way she could get him up there without his help. Simon seemed to sense the importance of staying conscious and shook his head, as if to wake himself up.

It worked. He looked at her, clear-eyed, and said, "I'm ready. I can do this."

The water level kept pace with every upward step they took, so they constantly fought the power of the water. It took them five minutes before they were above the water level, and another five to reach the ledge. Simon passed out as soon as they were safe. Cat admired his self-control. The climb wasn't easy for him in his condition, yet somehow he had willed himself to stay conscious.

The water level was about five feet below the ledge and seemed to have peaked. Cat looked around. Through the pelting rain, she could make out the two horses in the forest on the other side of the gorge, well above the water level. They were safe.

Cat was freezing. She was soaked to the skin. She moved over to the unconscious Simon and snuggled close to him, being careful of his arm. She knew about hypothermia. The closer they could get, the better chance they had of staying warm.

She fell asleep by his side.

*****

She awoke to sunshine. The water was still flowing

steadily, although the level had dropped considerably, but she was now being treated to the warm rays of the sun. She was shivering from the cold and wet, but knew the sun would soon take the chill away. The ledge was sheltered from the breeze, maximizing the full effects of the sun.

Simon was still unconscious, but he was breathing. Cat took another look at him. He didn't seem close to waking. He probably needed the sleep, but she was worried about his wet clothes. Unfortunately, there wasn't anything she could do about Simon. She could get dry herself, though. She just had to take off her clothes and lay them out in the sun. It would also give the sun the chance to get warmth directly into her chilled body. She glanced again at the sleeping Simon. He needed his wet clothes taken off. Cat tried to wake him up, but when he didn't respond, she gave up. She wasn't sure what else she could do to help him. Simon was facing away from her. Cat peeled off her jacket, shirt, and t-shirt and laid them out in the sun. Then she took off her boots, socks, pants, and—hesitating at first—her underwear.

Suddenly, all of the feelings of desire she had been having bubbled to the surface. It was exciting! Exciting and a little dangerous. What if Simon woke up and saw her? A year ago, she could have stripped without giving it a second thought. You do what you have to do, and if that was what she had to do to avoid hypothermia, she wouldn't have hesitated. It wouldn't have mattered who was around. It was the logical thing to do. Her mother would have disapproved though. She would have said it was inappropriate to take off her clothes in front of others—especially boys. Cat had never understood that thinking. You do what you have to do to survive. Animals understood that.

But it was different now. She pulled her knees up to her body and hugged them—embarrassed by her feelings. After a few moments though, it was clear that Simon wasn't going to wake up any time soon, so she slowly relaxed and laid flat to let the sun's rays catch her. Already, she could feel the sun at work warming her body. She fell asleep again.

She awoke with a start. Simon was stirring. Cat quickly scooped up her underwear, pants and t-shirt and put them on, leaving the rest of her clothes on the ledge to continue drying. The clothes she put on were damp, but better than they had been earlier.

Simon sat up, still facing away. When he turned toward her, he looked first in her face before looking around at the surroundings. It was almost as if ... and it hit her. He wasn't just now waking up. He had already woken up and had seen her there naked! He was just being polite, making the "waking up noise" to warn her. How long had he been awake? How long had he been looking at her? Another wave of excitement shot through her, then a sense of appreciation for the way he had handled it.

"You might want to take your shirt off to dry," she said. She stumbled badly trying to get the sentence out. She almost said "shirt and pants." While it was logical that he should take off his pants to dry, she couldn't come out and say it.

Simon tried to take off his jacket, but cried out when he moved his bad arm. Cat scrambled to her feet to help him. Together, they took off his jacket, then unbuttoned his shirt and slipped it off. She laid them out next to her own clothes. Simon sat down in obvious pain. Cat looked at his arm. His forearm had a bump in it and had turned black and blue. There was nothing she could do until the waters receded and she could get to Scooby. She had a first-aid kit in her saddlebags. Using some string from the kit and a piece of wood from the forest, she could splint the arm.

Cat sat across from Simon and couldn't help but to stare at his upper body. He was skinny ... so skinny. His arms were thin and his chest was almost sunken. He caught her looking at him and quickly picked up his shirt with his good arm and covered himself.

Cat recovered and gave him a smile. "I'm sorry," she said. "I didn't mean to stare."

He slowly put his shirt back on the rock, but was clearly self-conscious now.

"Why are you so skinny?"

Cat's mom and dad had often warned her about being so direct, that sometimes it made people uncomfortable. But she didn't understand that. If you had a question, what was wrong with asking it?

But this time she had hit a nerve and she regretted her directness. Simon was looking away. When he turned back toward her, she saw tears in his eyes.

"Are you going to laugh too?"

She cocked her head. "Why would I laugh?"

"It's okay. I'm used to it."

And then she understood. She had seen some of the kids at school making fun of other kids for stupid reasons—reasons that didn't make sense to her. A skinny boy would probably get teased a lot. Maybe he was teased where he lived before.

"I'm sorry. Sometimes I ask questions I shouldn't ask. But

I'm really just curious. I don't mean anything by it."

"Are you serious?"

"I'm always serious. My mom says I'm too serious. I can't help it. You don't have to answer if you don't want to."

"No, that's okay. I don't mind."

Before starting his story he adjusted his position against the rock to make himself more comfortable—a losing effort.

"I was sick. I was born sick. My mom and dad say I almost died. Where I lived before, we didn't have a doctor, so nobody knows what made me sick or what I had. My parents just did the best they could. We lived in a place that got really cold in the winter, with a lot of snow. It wasn't good for my health and my parents wanted to move further south, but I was just wasn't well enough. I know it was really hard on my parents."

"Did you have to stay in the house? Did you go to school?"

"My mom taught me at home. In the warm weather I could go outside, but I couldn't really do anything. I could walk, but not much else. I just didn't have the strength. I couldn't play with the other kids, so I had no friends."

"What did you do?"

"I spent a lot of time in the woods. I read. I watched the birds, squirrels, foxes, and other animals."

Cat could relate, and told him so.

"I love nature," he said. "It's so quiet and peaceful." He lowered his voice. "I like animals better than people."

Cat nodded in response, waiting for him to finish his story.

"Three years ago I started to get better. I wasn't as healthy as other kids, but my parents thought it was time for me to go to school. I know they meant well, but I hated it. I still couldn't do everything the other kids could do, and they knew it. They made fun of me." He tailed off.

"Why do they do that?" asked Cat. "My mom and dad told me that in the old world people were often mean to each other. They don't understand it when people are mean now. They say that in the new world, there should be no place for it."

"I wish."

"I know. Some of the kids here can be bullies. I stay away from them."

Simon chuckled. "I bet they stay away from you. I wouldn't want to mess with you." He got serious. "So I can expect the same thing from the kids here." It was said as a statement.

Cat stared at him, deep in thought. Simon, not sure of the meaning behind the stare, finally looked away.

"Can you shoot?" Cat asked.

"Why? You want me to shoot someone?"

But Cat's serious side had kicked in and she didn't get the joke. She waited for the answer.

"A little bit. My dad tried to teach me. Early on, I was just too weak, but as I got stronger, my dad admitted that he wasn't very good himself. He did his best. He's a big guy and can do a lot of things, but he's not very good with guns. He's trying to help me build my strength, but he says it's going to take a while. He says that because of my illness, I'm just behind others. Of course, my broken arm will slow that down."

"We have a month before school starts," Cat said. "I can't help you with your strength, but I can teach you to shoot. By the time school starts, you'll be better than any of them when it comes to shooting a pistol. I'll teach you shoot it one-handed. And when your arm is better, I'll teach you the rifle. I'll even teach you the crossbow, if you want."

"How do you know I'll be better than the others?"

"Because I'm better than any of them."

Simon watched her eyes and her face. She wasn't kidding. But she also wasn't bragging. In the very short time he had known her, he realized that she was very simple in her approach to life. She told it like it was. He doubted she was capable of bragging or of lying. Her outlook on life had been heavily influenced by the animal kingdom.

"Okay," he said. "You've got a deal."

And the friendship between Cat and Simon was born.

Chapter 12

From that point on, Cat and Simon were inseparable. Their shared love of nature had them exploring areas of Yellowstone Cat hadn't found on her own. Since Cat and Simon had both grown up as loners, both sets of parents were relieved that their children had each found a close friend in the other.

The first couple of months of their friendship were spent impatiently waiting for Simon's broken arm to heal. The town's doctor had set it and made a cast for it, so extra care had to be taken in most areas, such as horseback riding. Simon's father gave him a pistol to practice with, once Ben and Lila assured him that Cat knew what she was doing and would make an excellent teacher. Simon spent hours practicing shooting one-handed, and by the time school started, he was quite proficient.

Maybe it was spending time with Cat, or maybe Simon was naturally developing his own sense of confidence. Whatever the reason, their fears of Simon being bullied by the other kids were unfounded. He was well-liked from the start and was seen as Cat's counterpart. It became obvious to the other teens that Cat and Simon, although liked and respected, were both a bit *different*. They all knew that Cat was unusual in her loner preference, and now to find someone almost just like her was viewed by the others with amusement.

But Cat and Simon weren't exactly alike, which might have been why they connected so easily. They liked the same things, but were different in approach. Cat, having spent her early years with animals as her only friends, saw herself as not much different than the animals she observed and interacted with on a daily basis. As such, she was direct in her speech and saw little need for tact, despite being kind and thoughtful in her own way. Simon, on the other hand, had always observed nature from afar, either from his bedroom or from his perch in the yard. His friends were books—novels, animal guidebooks, books of history, self-help books—anything that struck a chord with him. As such, Simon related more to people—despite spending little time around them due to his physical condition.

Over time, because of Simon, Cat began to learn how to relate to people in a more *human* way and, because of Cat, Simon was able to come face to face with the animal world in a way he could only wish for when he was younger.

Simon's body strengthened over time. Spending at least a part of almost every day exploring the countryside with Cat allowed his lungs to develop and his health to improve. They didn't know if his chest would ever be muscular like the other males living in Yellowstone, but that was of little concern to him or to Cat. The fact that he was becoming healthy was much more important.

At first, despite Cat's changing body and emerging sexual urges, there was no romantic feeling between them. They just loved to hang out together—they were true friends. However, over time, as Simon's body began to develop and his emotions and desires followed suit, things changed between them.

It was a year after they first met. They were sitting on a mountaintop in the western mountains of Yellowstone, overlooking a vista neither could ever tire of.

"Do you ever wonder what it was like for our parents growing up?" asked Simon.

"What do you mean?" asked Cat. She was only half listening. Her emotions were starting to get the best of her. Over the past few weeks, she had begun to see Simon in a different light. She was sure the feeling was mutual, but Simon had yet to make a move.

"They grew up with people all around them. Thousands of people all the time. Can you imagine that?"

"Never. I don't even like having a dozen people around me. You know, my mom was only a year older than I am now when the world changed. What I have trouble imagining is going from that kind of life to this kind of life overnight."

It was time to make things happen. Her hand moved slowly along the smooth rock toward Simon's hand. He seemed oblivious, but was he?

"Have your parents told you about their experiences?" asked Simon.

"They never used to, but last year they decided I was old enough. I can't believe some of the things they went through."

"My mom said everyone had heard of your parents. They were almost like legends."

"Yeah, I heard that too. They told me they were just in the right place at the right time."

Okay, enough was enough. Cat slowly touched Simon's hand, starting with his fingertips and finally putting her hand over his. He shifted uncomfortably, crossing his legs, but his hand responded. He turned it over and interlaced his fingers with hers. He looked her in the eyes. His face was red and beads of sweat had formed on his forehead.

Cat leaned over and kissed him lightly on the lips. He responded awkwardly, but tenderly, and then put his arms around Cat and held her tightly while they kissed.

"Wow," said Simon when they came up for air. "Wow."

"You already said that."

"Can I say it again?"

"Okay."

"Wow."

"I agree."

They kissed again, more comfortably this time. Finally, they sat back with the rock ledge behind them. Simon's arm was around Cat's shoulders and her head was resting against his chest.

"Do you remember when we first met last year and you saved me from the flood?" asked Simon.

"I didn't save you. We saved ourselves."

"Well anyway, we made it up onto that ledge and we both fell asleep?"

"Uh huh." Cat knew what was coming and she felt a surge of excitement course through her body.

"I woke up when you were sleeping and saw you naked."

"I thought so."

"I was … I don't know … fascinated, I guess. I didn't have the same kinds of feelings that I do now." He grinned. "Probably a good thing I didn't. But I liked that you were naked."

"How long were you looking at me?"

"A long time. Twenty minutes, at least. Long enough to memorize every inch of you."

Cat blushed.

"Over the last year, as I started having feelings for you, I've thought about that time over and over."

"I'll bet you have."

It was Simon's turn to blush.

"Anyway," he said hoarsely, suddenly needing water, "I just wanted to tell you that."

"I'm glad."

The afternoon sun was warm, and they dozed, snuggled in each other's arms.

*****

Cat woke up first. It was dark and there was a horrible smell in the air. Could it be night already? And then it hit her. It wasn't night. The blackness was smoke! She jumped up, rousing Simon in the process. He was instantly awake.

"Forest fire!" said Cat as calmly as she could. This was no time to panic. She had to think logically. The memories flooded in of the fire that drove them from their home in the mountains back east years before—scary memories. "We have to get out of here."

"Which way is it coming from?" asked Simon. Cat could tell that he was also thinking clearly. Determine its direction before making any decisions.

Burning embers were blowing in with the smoke. One landed on Cat's arm. She cried out in pain. "It's coming from the west," she said, with tears in her eyes from the burn on her arm. The horses were tied on the eastern side of the rock they were on. If the horses hadn't become untied, they still had a chance. Flames were going to sweep over the ledge any minute.

They climbed down the rocks and found the horses scared, but still there. They untied them and jumped into their saddles. The fire was only minutes from overtaking them. They found the trail they had come in on and headed east, back toward home. They were many miles from home, but Cat knew how quickly these fires could move.

"We have to warn everybody," cried out Simon over the roar of the approaching fire.

"I'm sure they've seen the smoke," replied Cat.

They rode for about two miles, when suddenly Cat reined in Scooby. Simon stopped beside her.

"What's wrong?" he asked.

"Feel that?"

He wasn't sure at first what she was talking about. And then he felt it.

"We're going into the wind. The wind has completely changed direction."

In fact, it was a stiff wind blowing back toward the west. A rumble sounded.

"Thunder," said Cat. She looked up at the sky. They had outrun the smoke, but now the blackness she saw belonged to clouds. "We're going to get dumped on. I've never been so happy to see rain."

"The wind is blowing the fire back the way it came," said Simon. "It will lose its energy. Add to that the rain and it should be extinguished altogether."

As the rain began to fall, they found a thick overhang of branches and got off their horses, tying the reins to one of the lower branches. They dug out ponchos from their saddlebags and sat against a tree to wait out the storm. They held hands.

"This day sure changed in a hurry," said Simon. "And yet, here we are, still holding each other. How's your arm?"

"It hurts, but I don't think it's all that bad."

Simon got up and retrieved a first aid kit from his saddlebag.

"Let me see it."

Cat held her arm out and Simon washed the burn with water from his canteen and some soap from his saddlebag and wrapped it in gauze.

"It's not too bad, but I bet it hurts."

"Feels a little better now."

The storm was violent, as so many of them were, and lasted a couple of hours before finally dying out. By then it was early evening and the sun was going down.

"It'll be too dangerous to ride in the dark," said Cat. "I think we should camp here and go home in the morning."

"Our parents will be worried."

"Maybe, but I think this is the smart thing to do."

"I agree. I'll find some rocks to put around a campfire."

"I'll try to find some dry wood."

In an hour, they had a good fire going, warming them after the rain had cooled everything down. Their sleeping bags—a necessity to have with them anytime they went riding—were pretty dry, but they laid them next to the fire to get the dampness out. They dug into their saddlebags for food and came out with some smoked fish and fresh vegetables, including carrots, which they fed to the horses.

The forest fire and subsequent rain storm had tired them out, and they fell asleep fairly early, fully clothed and lying in each other's arms.

*****

The sun was already well up in the sky when they woke up to the sound of approaching horses. Just to be safe, they pulled their rifles from the scabbards and waited. But they needn't have worried. From around a bend came Cat's parents, Simon's parents, and Aaron and Sean. They all looked relieved to see Cat and Simon, and they jumped off their horses and gave the kids hugs.

Simon built up the fire and boiled water for tea. Then the teens told them the story of the previous day.

"I wasn't worried," said Ben. "I knew you were both capable enough to get out of its way."

"You weren't worried?" said Lila. "Then why were you awake all night?"

Ben shrugged it off while the others laughed. The truth was, they were all worried.

"Do you have any idea what started it?" asked Sean. "Lightning?"

"No," answered Cat. "The storm didn't hit until long after the fire started. We were napping on a high ledge and didn't wake up until the fire was almost on us."

Lila noticed that Cat and Simon were holding hands. She looked over at Simon's mother, Linnea, who gave her a knowing smile. They knew it was bound to happen at some point.

"I don't know how it would start if it wasn't a lightning strike," said Sean. "I'd like to see if I can figure it out."

"Let's all go together," said Ben.

They put out the campfire and headed west. They went a couple of miles before they began to see the effects of the fire. When they reached the ledge Cat and Simon had been on, the two teens looked at each other with a tinge of sadness. The whole rock was now black, and the beautiful scene that they had been looking out on was gone. Smoke hung heavy in the air as they rode through the blackened forest. Ahead, they could see an unblemished valley.

"I think we are reaching the other side of it," said Sean.

"If the wind hadn't changed direction," said Cat, "we would have lost a lot more than we did."

"I used to curse the storms," said Ben. "Not anymore."

They emerged from the woods into the valley and turned around to see if they could get a sense of what started the fire.

"Let's spread out," said Aaron, "and see if something presents itself."

It took less than ten minutes.

"Over here," said Lila, looking down at a pile of charred wood.

"Here," said Simon.

"And here," said Sean.

The three spots were almost identical. Wood had been piled near some thickets. The wood was charred, but still recognizable. The wind had blown the flames into the forest and eventually the fire on the wood had died out.

"This was set," said Ben.

Meanwhile, Cat had gone further into the charred remains of the forest, concerned as usual that the animals had made it out safely. Up ahead she saw a body. It was large like a deer. As she got closer, she knew it wasn't a deer. She looked down and inhaled sharply.

"Over here." She had to say it twice, as the first time it caught in her throat.

In a minute they were all there. Ben, Aaron, and Sean got off their horses and examined the body.

It was a man. He had heavy burns on his body, but he was still recognizable. Ben estimated his age at around sixty, wearing overalls, and he had the remains of what had been a long beard. He had been burned alive, based on the expression on his face. His mouth was wide open, showing only a half dozen teeth.

"Look familiar?" said Aaron.

"You think it's one of the people who killed Clete?" asked Ben.

"You saw one of them. Did he look like this?"

"Yeah."

"Which means what?" asked Simon's father, Mike.

"It means they are travelling," said Ben. "They wouldn't have started a fire for nothing. I think they know we're here."

"How would they know that?"

"They tortured Clete. He probably told them whatever they wanted to know."

"These people are going to be a problem," said Lila. "A real problem."

Part Two: The Migration

Chapter 13

Seventeen years. It was sometimes hard to believe that the world I used to know had ended seventeen years earlier. Many of those years had been hard, but there were no regrets. I didn't miss my old life. It was a noisy world … a sick world. It was falling apart at the seams. There was just too much hatred and ugliness. Granted, wiping out most of the population might have been an extreme solution to the problem, but in its own twisted way, it worked. Healing was in full swing. Although it took some longer than others, most of the adults in the new society had adapted well. The kids didn't know any other life. Any problems they may have had with the new world were our fault. Their kids would be the most well-adjusted citizens of the new world. They wouldn't have to worry about their parents coming to grips with everything new. And the world itself was healing. The cities were still there, although overgrown and quiet, but many of the smaller towns had virtually disappeared, having given up the fight to the blossoming of the earth.

It's because I remembered the old world so clearly that I had little tolerance for the bad elements in life—the groups Lila and I ran across after the event and on our journey west, as well as the group we almost encountered during our search for Sophie.

I was a farmer and a rancher now, perfectly content to stay close to home tending to my crops and animals—except when I wasn't. I had helpers. Cat and Simon would split their time between our place and Simon's parents' homestead, doing whatever chores were needed. That allowed me the freedom to take off on two- and three-day journeys of exploration. Sometimes I'd go alone and sometimes Lila would accompany me, and we would recapture some of the good memories of our days hiking the Appalachian Trail on our odyssey south after the event.

Lila didn't share my love of farming and ranching, however. She had become one of the movers and shakers of the Yellowstone community. She was respected for her common sense and her abilities as a problem-solver. She spent many of her days in the town of Rock Creek organizing community events and developing a healthy town government.

Simon had grown strong and healthy, no resemblance whatsoever to the sickly boy who arrived in Yellowstone just two years earlier. He was a kind and gentle soul, very much like a son to us. Cat, now sixteen, and the spitting image of Lila at that age, had softened a bit—still serious, but less so. She had learned to laugh and to see the humor in things—thanks to Simon. She and Simon were a devoted couple. According to Lila, who had "those" types of discussions with our daughter, Cat and Simon hadn't yet had sex. That made me happy. There would be a lot of time for that. The devotion they had for each other was based on the love of nature they shared, and the kindness each possessed toward every living creature, from humans on down.

I will admit to being a little puzzled by Cat's decision to leave home with the group of other teens. Her leaving wasn't what puzzled me, it was her decision to join the group. If she had come to us and announced that she and Simon were heading out on their own, I wouldn't have considered that strange at all. In fact, Lila and I were preparing ourselves for that possibility. But Cat was a loner, as was Simon, and while she had known most of those kids for years, she wasn't overly close to any of them. So I had to ask. Her answer made sense in a way typical of her common-sense outlook on life. "There is security in a group," she said. "But Simon and I will stay with the group for only as long as we need them or they need us. If we are drawn to an area they aren't, that's when we will part company. They understand, and probably know we won't stay with them the whole way." It made sense to me, but then, that wasn't unusual. Cat looked at life logically.

We didn't know how long they would be gone, or if they'd even be back, but we would miss them terribly. We also knew that our life would change dramatically, and that saddened me. But I was able to be happy for them and the adventures they had in store for themselves. Lila and I could relate. So all we could do was wish them well and try not to think about the hole their leaving was going to put in our hearts.

Chapter 14

They left on a beautiful summer day. There were twelve of them altogether, ranging in age from fourteen to nineteen. The oldest was Zack and the youngest was Darcy, the only fourteen-year-old in the group. Most of the parents wouldn't have considered allowing a fourteen-year-old to take such a trip, but Darcy, like her single mother, had the reputation of being a bit wild. For Ben and Lila, it felt like Sophie all over again, but there was nothing they could do. The school of thought was that the mother had encouraged her daughter to be part of the group in order to give the mother the freedom to pursue her lifestyle with the handful of single men who regularly stopped by. Already, Darcy—who looked older than her fourteen years—was following in her mother's footsteps by having two of the seven males in the group showing more than a little interest in her.

The plan was devised six months earlier in the dead of winter. While it was a group decision to go, it was Zack who suggested it. They were having a youth group meeting in Rock Creek, a popular bi-weekly event organized by Lila that was regularly attended by over thirty teens. Part of every meeting was an open discussion—any topic was accepted.

At this particular meeting—held soon after a three-day snowstorm—the teens were discussing what was beyond the borders of Yellowstone. Most had never explored more than a few miles in any direction, Cat and Simon being the exceptions. Although many of them had traveled across the country to get to Yellowstone when they were young, very few remembered much about the trip. They had heard all of the stories from their parents about life before the event. Now, they were itching to experience the world for themselves. For six months they discussed, planned, and put into motion the trip. At first, twenty-five of the thirty teens expressed an interest, but that number got whittled down by a number of factors. Some parents said an emphatic "no" to the idea, and a couple of the teens were voted down due to their age (and yet, Darcy somehow made the cut—an irony not lost on the other female members of the group). A few of them chickened out as the date drew closer. So, a month before they left, the list was frozen at twelve.

Since Zack was the oldest and largest of the group, and since it was his idea in the first place, he became the leader by default. Cat and Simon were curious to see how long it would take for his lack of experience in the wilderness to kick in and dampen his leadership enthusiasm. His second-in-command, so to speak, was Morgan, a tall, lanky 18-year-old. Cat didn't like Morgan. He had hit on her a year earlier—knowing full well of her committed relationship with Simon. In fact, of all the teens in Yellowstone, he was the only one who looked at Simon with disdain. Needless to say, he had now switched his attention and effort (not that it took much) toward Darcy, who returned the attention enthusiastically.

And then there were the 17-year-old twins, William and Harry. They were named after some English princes from before the event—Cat had never heard of them.

The two that Cat and Simon were closest to in the group were also loners. Wade, at sixteen, was the only black teen in Yellowstone. There were a few other black young people, but none of them had yet reached their teens. Although racism had long since died in what was left of the country, Wade occasionally confided to Cat and Simon that he felt *different* at times. It made sense then that his best friend—and most likely future mate—was Yuki, the daughter of Japanese parents. Her parents had been part of a school trip of Japanese students from Tokyo visiting the States. The event occurred when they were in Chicago, and Yuki's parents were the only two teenagers from the tour to survive the event. Naturally, they stuck together, eventually becoming lovers and giving birth to Yuki. Her parents spoke very little English at first, and even seventeen years later were still uncomfortable speaking it, but they had picked up enough to communicate with others well enough. The family spoke only Japanese at home, but Yuki spoke only English—without any trace of a Japanese accent—outside of the home.

The final three teens in the group were Emma, Diana, and John, all seventeen. Cat knew them as well as she knew any of the others, but had never formed any kind of relationship with them. They were all nice and—more importantly to Cat—capable of taking care of themselves.

Their proposed route was the source of numerous arguments, though not among the teens. The source of the conflict originated with the parents. The original plan called for the group to head directly west, eventually reaching the Pacific. None of them—not even Cat—had ever been told the full story of Clete and Sophie. All they knew was that the couple had been found dead. Ben and Lila had sat them all down and had tried to explain the situation delicately, holding back as many of the facts as they could. The parents were assured by the teens that they'd be careful and that the parents had nothing to worry about. The conversation got heated. In the end it was no use. They had to come clean with the teens.

By that time, Ben and Lila had decided that if the kids were old enough to take such a journey, they were old enough to hear the truth. Ben, having been at the scene of both deaths, told the story. He left nothing out. When he finished, there was complete silence in the room. Some of the kids wore stunned expressions. At that point in the process, there had been fourteen participants. After Ben's story, two of the young men bowed out.

Once it was agreed that changing course was the prudent thing to do, the conversation turned productive. Morgan suggested heading east, but was shot down immediately. Even though most of the teens were too young to remember a lot of the details of their trip to Yellowstone, they had all come from the east. Somehow, going back in that direction didn't feel new.

They finally settled on a southerly route. Judging by the note written on Clete's body stating the land as belonging to the group that killed him, Ben felt the group was settled well west of Yellowstone. Even though there had been evidence of them reaching the western border of the park, he doubted their territory extended much further south than that.

If the teens headed due south from Yellowstone, they would probably be safe from the group that killed Clete. Their route would eventually take them through Salt Lake City to Las Vegas, where they would turn west toward the ocean. The subject of how long the trip would take was avoided. No one knew. They could turn back in a month or return in a couple of years. Since no one had a clue, it was better not discussed.

*****

A large segment of the Yellowstone population gathered in Rock Creek to see the teens off. There were tears and lots of hugging. Cat and Simon tried hard not to cry, but lost the battle when they saw the tears flowing from their parents. Looking around, Cat noticed most of the others having the same problem. The only two who appeared to be unaffected by the emotions of the moment were Morgan and Darcy.

The goodbyes lasted longer than any of them had expected. As a result, their planned early morning departure was delayed almost three hours. At the urging of Zack and Morgan, the explorers finally detached themselves from their families and got on their way. The planned route south took them along the remains of a seasonal highway that wound its way through the mountains. Zack led the way, followed closely by Morgan and Darcy. William, Harry, Emma, John, and Diana were bunched together in the middle, talking excitedly about the trip ahead. Following almost a hundred yards behind were Yuki and Wade, with Cat and Simon bringing up the rear. The four in the back of the group said very little for the first couple of hours, instead just observing the surroundings. Cat and Simon had never traveled the southern route, so they wanted to take the time to appreciate the country.

Occasionally, the road was broken by a crevasse. The group was forced to go around each one—sometimes traveling many miles before they found a crossover point. As a result, the first day they made it less than twenty miles.

They camped for the night beside a small stream. Knowing they'd have to hunt and fish for most of their food on the journey, the group had packed food in advance for the first couple of days. William and Yuki built a fire while the others set up tents. Despite their relationship not yet reaching the pinnacle of intimacy, Cat and Simon had decided to share a tent. Being brothers, William and Harry also shared one. There was no doubt that Wade and Yuki would share a tent as well. All of the others had single tents, although no one expected Darcy to ever be alone in hers.

Other than Morgan, the group turned out to be quite harmonious. By the end of the second day, Cat felt she knew most of the others fairly well. John, Diana, and Emma all surprised her, each showing a great enthusiasm for the trip and a good knowledge of woodsmanship. William and Harry both showed signs of homesickness, but persevered nonetheless. Wade and Yuki—true to form—were quiet, but both were skilled in the ways of the land and proved themselves indispensable to the group. Zack was taking his job as leader seriously, but he was always pleasant and wasn't afraid to solicit suggestions from the others. Even Darcy turned out to be fun. The least mature of the group—despite her advanced sexual prowess—she had a good sense of humor that Cat had never seen in her before.

The only potential problem in the group was Morgan. Cat, who had lived among the animals all of her life and had picked up an animal's ability to sense danger, definitely felt it emanating from Morgan. The second oldest of the group, he spent a lot of his time with Zack, trying to assert his presence and opinions. By the end of the third day, even Zack was tiring of Morgan and spent less time talking to him. That would cause Morgan to ride off alone for an hour or two, meeting up with the group a few miles down the road.

The only one not tired of Morgan was Darcy. To her, Morgan possessed a manly quality that Zack, despite being older, lacked. Although smaller than Zack, Morgan was more experienced in the woods and—more importantly—talked himself up more effectively. As a result, by the end of the first week, it was clear that Darcy and Morgan had an exclusive sexual arrangement. Zack then turned his interest to Emma and Diana, both of whom were flattered at Zack's attention, but having seen Zack with Darcy, were cautious about getting involved with him.

They occasionally ran across the remains of a small mountain town—most not much larger than a gas station, a general store, and a few houses. The towns provided little interest to them, however, due to their advanced states of dilapidation. Most of the buildings had collapsed from a combination of the earthquake and the years of severe weather.

That changed when they emerged from the hills into a large valley and a town called Jackson. The sign at the entrance to the town said it was Jackson, Wyoming, but other than having learned about states in school, the "Wyoming" part meant very little to them. For that matter, so did the "Jackson" part. For every member of the group, a town was nothing more than a curiosity. Having heard all the stories about the earthquakes that hit each part of the country, and having experienced the severe weather their whole lives, none of them really expected to find a town that was intact enough to be worth exploring.

Jackson turned out to be a complete surprise. Although many of the buildings had fallen in on themselves, there were still a few that were intact. Some of the buildings were made of stone—at least partially—which had given added support to the wooden upper structures and roofs. Those buildings that were still intact weren't clean by any means. Plant growth was rampant, having grown up through the floors of the buildings. In some cases, trees had pushed themselves out of window openings. Rusted vehicles littered the streets. Any remains of human bodies were long since gone.

It was strange. As excited as they were to find a town they could explore, there was something almost creepy about it. They had read about ghost towns in school, and Jackson fit the bill. It was quiet and it was dead. It was obvious that at one time it had been a pretty town, but they really had to use their imaginations to picture it that way. The teens spoke quietly to each other as they rode through the empty streets. Talking loudly seemed somehow wrong. A wind had come up, only adding to the spookiness.

"Look at the roads," said Cat in a low voice to the others. "No cracks. The earthquake somehow missed this town. That's why more buildings weren't destroyed."

They dismounted in front of a large store whose faded sign advertised gifts. Getting into the building proved impossible though, as the growth was just too dense. They walked their horses down the street, looking into each building they passed. Finally, they ran across one that seemed to have escaped the plant growth. That one, as well, advertised gifts.

"It seems like they all sold gifts," said Wade. "I've got to see what all the excitement was about."

They broke down the front door and slowly filed in, being mindful of weak and broken boards under them. Cat picked up a ceramic statue of a person on skis. A sign next to the person said, *Jackson Hole, WY.*

"What possible use could this have had?" she asked.

"I think people brought them home as reminders of where they'd been," said Zack.

"Why?"

"My dad said they called things like that souvenirs."

"I don't get it," said Cat.

"People liked to travel. It helped people remember."

Cat shook her head. "They couldn't remember in their own brain? It doesn't make sense."

"Sense or not," said Simon, "There are thousands of these things in here. And if the other stores had as many as this store has, a lot of people wanted to remember this place."

"I wonder why," said Cat. "It's just a town."

They all lost interest quickly and left the building. They wandered through the town for another hour or so, only breaking into one other building. The sign advertised camping and skiing equipment and was not too heavily overgrown. Disappointment set in when they discovered how rusted all the metal items were and how rotted much of the cloth was. However, Morgan found a cabinet filled with boxes containing knives of all sizes. The knives on display had rusted, but those in the boxes were still in fairly good shape. They each grabbed a variety of knives for their saddlebags.

Finally it was time to leave. It was late afternoon and they would need to find a place to camp for the night—and none of them wanted to camp in town. Directly south of the town it was still part of the valley. Having grown up in Yellowstone, they were all more comfortable—and felt less vulnerable—in the hills, so the group moved into the hills off to the left of the valley and found a flat spot among the rocks to set up camp.

Later, around the fire, they discussed what they had seen in Jackson.

"It was a strange place," said Cat.

"The town?" asked Emma.

"The world."

No one said anything, so she continued.

"The things they gave importance to. I'm still amazed at all of those pieces of junk. I don't understand it."

"The world was a lot different," said Simon.

"No shit," said Morgan.

"What I mean is, people had everything they needed in life. They didn't have to fend for themselves. I've read quite a bit about it. There was a lot of stress and a lot of anxiety, and so they spent as much time as possible going to different places to get away from home."

He got a lot of puzzled looks.

"I know. It doesn't make sense. They had everything they needed. But I think that was part of the problem. Everything was too complicated. We've all heard our parents talk about the past and the things they miss from that life. But I think they've all admitted that life is less stressful now. And most of them were about our age when the event happened. If they were stressed, imagine what it was like for their parents."

"Old man Murphy, who must be like, seventy or something, told me that life was pretty good back then," said Zack. "I think he still misses it. So I guess not everyone was stressed."

It was too much to think about, so they all headed to bed, not sure whether they were more excited or more disturbed to have found a fairly intact town. Part of this trip was to discover their roots—the world their parents once knew and had thrived in. After their experience in Jackson, they weren't totally sure anymore that they still wanted to find that world.

Chapter 15

It didn't take long for dissension in the ranks to set in.

As much as possible, they tried to follow the traces of the old highway, but they eventually had to give up. The further south they went, the more broken up the landscape became. Crevasses were a problem, but it was more than that. The ground was rough in so many places, it was often difficult footing for the horses.

They would stop mid-afternoon to set up camp for the night. It had always been their intention to stop early to give themselves time to hunt or fish for dinner, but mid-afternoon was much earlier than planned. However, the horses needed a break—as did their riders—due to the grueling journey.

The sun was setting on their most recent camp, this one at the edge of a small lake. Cat and Simon had volunteered to do the fishing that night and had returned with a dozen large fish. Her father had once told her that when he was young, many of the lakes and ponds—and even the ocean—had become so polluted, it was difficult to catch fish, and many of those they caught couldn't be eaten due to the poisons in the water. But over the years, he said, the earth seemed to be cleansing itself.

The fish were now plentiful and easy to catch. Cat had to take his word for the first part of the story, because she had only ever known abundant fishing.

Diana and John were the cooks for the night and had prepared a tasty meal with the fish and a variety of wild vegetables the group had collected along the way. Despite the good food, they all ate with little enthusiasm, and unlike most nights, there was little talking.

Morgan finally broke the silence.

"This sucks."

They all looked at him, waiting for the follow-up.

"Not the food. The trip. We weren't expecting this. We're going nowhere. It takes us hours to go a couple of miles. Forget making it to the ocean, I just want to make it to flat land."

"What do you suggest?" asked Zack.

"Look, we've been following this valley ever since we left the mountains. It made sense when we looked at the map. We've got mountains to the east of us and mountains to the west. This looked to be the quickest route south, but it's not. I think it would be easier and quicker to travel through the mountains. They didn't seem to get hit by the earthquake as badly as the flat areas did."

"Makes sense," said Emma. "And there are some old roads that wind their way through the mountains. I think we should take the chance."

"Are you still talking about heading west?" asked Simon.

"Of course," said Morgan.

"We weren't going to go west until we reached Salt Lake City," said Cat. "My dad said it would be too dangerous if we went before that."

"Ah yes. Ben, of the great and famous Ben and Lila. You know how sick of their story I am?"

Cat felt Simon stir beside her. She put her hand on his wrist to stop him from getting up. She looked at Morgan and didn't say a word. It wasn't hatred she was feeling toward him, but he had crossed a line and it was her intention to give him a warning before she pounced.

Morgan picked up on it immediately. He had never seen a look like that from a human before. It was threatening, but without emotion. He had run across that look once a few years earlier when he encountered a bear with her cub in the woods. No sound had come from the bear, but Morgan knew that if he had taken one step closer, the bear would have charged him and probably taken his head off.

The others observed the interaction between Cat and Morgan and no one said a word.

"No offense intended," Morgan said quietly, backtracking as much as he could, while still saving face. "I'm just frustrated. What I mean is, those people—whoever they are—are a hundred miles north of us and another couple of hundred west. They have their own place to live. They're not going to travel this far south."

"They traveled that far east," said Simon. "They started the fire at Yellowstone."

"We don't know for sure if that was them," said William. "I agree with Morgan. We should head west."

"I think we should go home," said his brother. "I'm tired of this. This isn't what I thought it would be. I don't think it's what any of us thought it would be. We're not finding our roots or discovering the past. What we're doing now, we could just as easily be doing at home."

"Shut up, Harry," said William. "You can't quit because it's a little hard going. We'll make it to the ocean and we'll see the cities. We'll learn our past."

"Really? You think so? You're so stupid. You say you want to see the cities, but look at how we all reacted in Jackson—and that wasn't even a city. We all felt uncomfortable and we couldn't wait to get out of there. And you want to go to a big city?"

"You want to go home?" said William. "Then go. No one is stopping you. Good riddance."

Cat realized that this wasn't a random outburst by the brothers. Harry had probably been complaining to William about the trip for a while. It bubbled to the surface with the argument between Morgan and her.

"Let's calm down," said Zack, trying to assert his leadership, but failing miserably. "We should talk about it."

"Where were you?" asked Morgan. "We just did. Now we need to make a decision. If we head east, we can forget about ever seeing the ocean. If we go west, maybe we'll meet up with the people who killed Clete, but what do we really know about them? We don't know how many there are. How many people does it take to kill one person? There are twelve of us, and some of us are damn good with a gun. There's safety in numbers. That's why we're doing this as a group. I say we go for it."

"I agree," said William.

"Okay," said Zack. Cat could see that he was seething inside at Morgan's verbal attack on him.

Cat looked over at Simon and shrugged.

"Okay," said Simon. "We're in."

From there, the rest of the group agreed to the new plan, except Harry, who was sulking.

"Harry?" asked William, now trying to sound sensitive.

"What the hell? I don't want to go back alone, so I guess I'll come."

After they ate, Cat and Simon took a walk around the lake.

"I see trouble coming between Zack and Morgan," said Simon.

"Zack is losing his position as leader," said Cat. "He's the oldest and it was his idea…"

"…and Morgan is positioning himself to take over," finished Simon. "Not a good situation. You know, we don't have to go with them. We can strike out on our own. I'm sure Wade and Yuki would join us."

"I was thinking of that. Morgan is right about this route. We can't continue on like this. One of our horses will break a leg. So maybe we should go with them for a while. When we feel the time is right, we can break off from the group."

That decision made, they held hands and just listened to the sounds of the animals as they walked.

*****

The next morning they started off toward the hills to the west. Within a few hours, they could already see a marked difference in the ease of travel as they entered more mountainous country. They found a trail. In actuality, it was once a road, evidenced by fallen down mile-markers. Now, like most roads in the country, it was covered with dirt and rocks.

Despite her earlier reservations, Cat was enjoying the new country they were travelling through. In general, the spirit of the group was much higher, with a few exceptions. Zack was no longer in front and had gone silent, resenting the fact that Morgan had, in effect, taken over the reins of leadership. Harry, too, had been quiet, riding in the back of the pack.

Even though Morgan now considered himself the leader, his following was small, basically William, Emma, and Darcy. Cat could tell that Diana and John were on the fence about him, especially as they were close to Zack. Harry, bringing up the rear, couldn't care less who was in charge. Wade and Yuki, like Cat and Simon, weren't willing to consider anyone else the leader. In their minds, they went where they liked.

There was even trouble in Morgan's own camp. Darcy and Morgan had been arguing all morning, and Cat noticed that Emma was now riding closer to Morgan. Simon mentioned it to Cat when they had drifted toward the rear and were alone.

"People have always thought I was a little strange because I avoid groups," Cat answered. "But this is why. I don't understand it. I don't understand how people relate to one another. With animals, it's simple."

"But animals don't have the same emotions as humans. In some ways, you have an animal mind in a human society. It's going to fall apart," he added. "The group, I mean."

"It's going to blow apart, not fall apart. When we agreed to this, I thought there would be safety in numbers, but I think I was wrong. I think we would have been better off just making a trip by ourselves."

"We might be doing that sooner than we thought."

They camped that night among rocks in the shadow of

some tall trees. Already, the difference in altitude made for cooler temperatures at night. Although the group was more animated, the undercurrents of tension were also evident, and the group had separated into three distinct segments. Darcy was now sitting with Zack, alone in a secluded corner. Wade and Yuki had joined Cat and Simon, with Harry hovering nearby. The remaining members sat with Morgan, listening to him expound on some subject. Morgan was obviously enjoying his new found position of power.

That night, based on the noise Cat and Simon could hear coming from Morgan's tent, and the fact that Emma's tent was empty, it was clear that the Morgan and Darcy relationship was officially over.

They continued west for several days, eventually reaching the town of Lava Hot Springs. Again, it looked to be a tourist town, with gift shops lining the street and the remains of swimming pools and water parks. Some of the spots had dried up when the earthquake shifted things around, but on the outskirts of the town they found a natural hot spring that had no tourist signs. Whether it was created by the earthquake or had already existed, they couldn't tell, but it gave them a spot to hunker down for a couple of days of rest.

The hot springs were glorious, and they took full advantage of them. When they weren't bathing, they poked around the town, which once again proved disappointing. The earthquake had hit the town hard and there was little to explore.

Zack and Harry went out hunting the first day and came back with a deer and bags of wild mushrooms and other wild plants. They spent three days in Lava Hot Springs, gorging on food and bathing in the springs.

*****

Cat and Simon spent time looking at the map during their three days of respite and had come to the conclusion that they wanted to turn south. They presented it to the group one night.

"We haven't checked out a real city yet," said Cat. "South of us is one called Salt Lake City. Simon and I would like to see it."

"There are cities west of here," said Morgan.

"No, there aren't, not until you reach the coast, and we don't even know where the coast is anymore. Nick and Jason said the coastline has probably changed. It could be a lot further inland than it used to be, and those cities might be gone. If we go down to Salt Lake City, it's probably still there to some degree. Nick and Jason also said that the Great Salt Lake is worth seeing. From there we can decide whether to go west or a little further south."

"Yuki and I agree," said Wade. "We're with you."

"I'll go with you," said Harry, who had begun to hang closer to Cat and Simon.

"I'm in," said Zack. He looked at Darcy by his side. "So is Darcy."

Diana and John looked conflicted, but finally Diana said, "John and I will come."

Morgan had a decision to make. If he agreed to go south with the group, how would he be seen by his two most loyal friends? John and Diana, who were on the fence to begin with, had made their choice.

"We'll come part of the way, then see how it goes," he said. Then he looked over at Zack, who was smirking, and said, "You gotta problem?"

"Nope." The smirk remained.

"I've had just about enough of you."

"Then leave."

Morgan jumped up and attacked Zack, who was sitting on a rock. As Zack rose, Morgan hit him full force with his body. The two went tumbling. Zack jumped to his feet and took a swing at Morgan. But the punch was too slow and Morgan smacked Zack in the face, Zack's punch ineffectively bouncing off Morgan's shoulder. Zack went down and was slow to get up.

"Knock it off," yelled Simon.

Morgan looked at Simon with hatred. "This is between me and him. Stay out of it."

Zack tackled Morgan as he was talking and they both went down in the dirt, slugging away. It only lasted another few seconds, as Cat, Simon, Wade, John, and William pulled the two apart.

The fight was over. Zack had definitely received the worst of it, and was bleeding from his nose and mouth. Morgan shrugged off the others, got up, and walked away.

"It ends here," said Cat.

"Go screw yourself," said Morgan.

"You want to try that again?" warned Simon.

"Seriously, Morgan," said William. "It ends here."

Morgan shrugged again and sat on the ground. Darcy was fussing over Zack, while shooting Morgan daggers with her eyes.

Morgan was the clear victor, and Cat wondered what it would do to Zack's self-esteem. She knew he was done trying to lead. For Morgan, it was a little different. He would continue to try to lead the group, but he also knew that Zack would get a lot of sympathy. Worse though, in his mind, than having Zack leading the group was Cat and Simon. Although they weren't trying to be in charge, Cat knew that a lot of the group was looking to them for a calm leadership, which was probably infuriating Morgan. He couldn't stand either one of them. But Cat knew he'd keep trying to assert himself. It was just who he was. His term in power didn't last very long the first time, but he'd gain the trust of some of them again. It would just be a matter of time.

They turned south the next morning. Morgan made sure he was leading the way, which didn't matter to Cat. She knew they had made the right decision to turn south. Emma rode with Morgan at the head of the group. Cat couldn't understand what she saw in Morgan, but she remembered her mother saying once that some women were attracted to "bad boys." Zack and Darcy were in the rear, far behind the others, talking to each other in low tones.

They traveled through mountainous terrain that would occasionally open up to long valleys. Unlike further north, however, the earthquake damage to the land was minimal, at least in terms of crevasses.

The one thing Cat noticed that she wasn't expecting—at least, according to the maps she had scoured—was that the flat land had become less prairie and more desert. She discussed it with Simon.

"My dad says that when the event happened, the weather

changed," said Simon. "What we've seen all our lives is very different from what our parents experienced."

"Yeah, my parents have said the same thing," said Cat.

"I think it's changed the land in a lot of ways."

"So prairie becomes desert," stated Cat.

"In some places. The further south we go, the more real desert we are going to find—desert that has always been there."

They stayed to the hills as much as possible, and a couple of days later hit the outskirts of Salt Lake City.

Chapter 16

It wasn't at all what they had expected. Up until that point, most of the towns they had run across were shells of what they had once been. Collapsed buildings and rampant vegetation made it difficult for them to imagine anyone ever having lived there.

Salt Lake City was different. Most of the buildings that they could see from their vantage point on a highway overpass seemed to be intact. And they were the tallest buildings any of them had ever seen. The highway on which they were standing was littered with vehicles of all shapes and sizes. They had seen a lot of cars on their journey to this point, but nothing like this. It was wall to wall vehicles. Most had long since rusted out and many—like the highway itself—were half covered in sand.

Cat remembered passing close to cities on their move west, as well as when she was kidnapped and taken to Paradise. But she had never seen anything like this.

"Everything is gray," said Simon.

"Do you think maybe it used to have colors and they've just disappeared over the years?" asked Emma.

"I don't think so. We've all seen pictures of cities in school.

The buildings were gray even then, but not like this."

"They had life," said Cat. "That's what made the difference."

"Let's go check it out," said Zack. "We should keep our guns handy, just in case."

It took them a lot longer than expected to reach the tall buildings. They passed through what seemed like miles of houses and stores. Some areas were overgrown and some seemed to have very little damage. Some of the outskirts had been hit hard by the earthquake, but the closer they got to the center of the city, the less damage they encountered.

"Are we going through lots of towns, or is this all part of the city?" asked Harry.

No one answered. No one had a clue.

By mid-afternoon they reached the center of the city. Other than the rusted, abandoned cars and the foot-deep layer of sand and salt over everything, it seemed untouched. There were lots of animal prints in the sand—mostly dogs—but no human footprints. They stopped in front of a tall, stark building.

"I want to go to the top," said Cat, peering into the sky and shading her eyes. "I want to see what they used to see."

"I'm with you," said Simon.

Darcy and Harry had no desire to explore the building, so they agreed to guard the horses. The others approached the front of the building. The glass doors and windows were long-since gone, so they walked into what was once the lobby.

"I wonder what it was," said Wade.

"I think it was what they called an office building" answered Simon. "People worked in it."

They found a stairwell and started their way up to the top.

Luckily, there were windows at each level, giving them enough light to keep climbing. At each landing they opened the door and peered down the hallway at the office doors. It was dark, but windows in the offices provided some light to see by.

"There must be a thousand rooms," said Yuki. "That means that thousands of people worked here. Hard to imagine. And it's so quiet. I'm trying to get a sense of what it might have been like, but I can't."

"Why would they all want to work in a place like this? What did they do?" asked William.

No one had an answer to the question.

They kept walking. They stopped checking out each floor when they realized they were all the same. Finally they reached the top. The sign read: "47th Floor." They opened the door. This floor was different from the others. It was sunnier, and it was all windows—almost all of which were unbroken. The whole floor was in the shape of a circle.

Unlike the outdoors, there were some skeletons remaining in the building that hadn't disappeared from the ravages of time, their clothes just disintegrating rags. Ignoring the skeletons, they moved as a group over to one of the windows and looked out.

"Wow!

"Unbelievable!"

They were looking over not just the whole city, but the whole valley. They went from one window to the next. From some they could see the mountains, and from others they looked across at a large body of water.

"The ocean?" asked Diana.

"The Great Salt Lake," said Wade. "Kind of like the ocean

because it's salt water. And that white area is salt. It's like a desert of salt."

"Someone was paying attention in school," said Yuki.

"What's that big building?" asked Cat.

"I think it's some kind of temple," answered Simon.

"Look at all the cars," said Morgan. "How could they get anywhere? It's like they're right on top of each other."

"Funny how I've looked down from mountaintops higher than this, but it looked different," said Cat.

"It's because this is straight up," said Simon. "Also, you've never looked down at a city before."

They stayed at least an hour. Finally, Morgan said, "The sun is beginning to go down and we haven't figured out where we're making camp tonight. It's going to take us a while to get down."

Cat moved away from the window, but as she did, she caught a glimpse of something out of the corner of her eye. She turned back. "I see something," she said.

The others crowded around as she pointed out toward the edge of the city, in the direction from which they had come.

"Looks like smoke."

Zack pulled binoculars from his backpack and zoomed in to the smoke.

"Too far away to get any details, but it looks like it might be a campfire."

"Should we check it out?" asked William.

"It's almost dark," said Morgan. "It would take us a couple of hours to get there even in the day. I say we should leave here and keep riding south as far as we can, then stop once it gets dark."

"I agree," said Cat. "Whoever they are seem to be coming from the same direction we came, and they are just a couple of hours behind us. That doesn't give me a good feeling. The more distance we get between us and them, the better."

It only took them a few minutes to make it down the forty-seven floors. Once down, they quickly filled in Harry and Darcy, then got on their way. Maneuvering the streets took a lot of time and just by luck they found themselves on the highway heading south. Skirting the dead cars was a lot easier than finding their way through the city. When the highway butted up against more mountainous terrain, they got off the road and headed east into the hills. By the time they picked out a campsite, darkness had fallen.

Everyone was exhausted from the day, so the meal was quick, with very little talking. Those who had gone up into the building were quietly reflecting on the experience, which was frustrating to Harry and Darcy, who had nothing but questions.

Cat and Simon had settled into their sleeping bags when Cat asked, "Do you think anyone lives there?"

"Where?"

"In Salt lake City. In any city, for that matter."

"I don't know. I guess I doubt it. What would be there for them?"

Cat was silent.

"I suppose they would have some comforts," Simon continued. "They could find a nice house with comfortable beds and the illusion of living in luxury, but what then? They could grow a garden for their vegetables, but what would they do for meat and fish? They'd have to hunt and the city isn't very well stocked. And then there is the winter. Where would they get their wood? In the beginning they'd raid the local parks for wood, but eventually that would run out. Doesn't make sense. Besides, we didn't see any footprints."

Simon was fidgeting as he talked.

"Are you okay?" asked Cat.

"No. There's been something I've wanted to say for a while, and now I need to say it."

"Uh oh."

"No, nothing like that. Cat, you and I have been together a couple of years. We do everything together and we're best friends. We're way more than best friends and I can't think of being with anyone else for the rest of my life." He hesitated. "But in all that time we've spent together, held each other, and kissed each other, I've never told you that I love you. I love you, Cat."

Cat looked at Simon and tears rolled down her cheeks. She reached out and pulled Simon to her and they just held each other. Finally they separated. She looked Simon in the eyes and said, "And I love you, Simon."

They hugged again and kissed, then laid down next to each other.

"Everyone thinks we're strange," said Simon.

"We are. We don't fit into society. People can't understand that."

"And yet, here we are at sixteen, and we know who we want to be with for the rest of our life. How many other people can say that?"

Cat rolled onto Simon and kissed him. Simon put his hands under her shirt and in a flourish, had it up and over her head.

"That was tricky," said Cat.

"I thought so. I've been practicing it in my head."

They kissed again, their hands exploring the other's body.

"Uh, Simon..."

"I know. We agreed to wait, and we will. I'm good with that. But I'm also okay with doing this."

"So am I. I was just checking."

An hour later, they fell asleep in each other's arms.

*****

They were all up early the next morning. Breakfast was a hurried affair and an hour after waking up, they were on the road.

"I think we should stick to our plan and head south toward Las Vegas, then turn west toward the ocean," said Zack.

He didn't encounter any disagreement. While no one knew who was behind them, or even if they were following them, the desire to put many miles between them and whoever was back there was on everybody's mind.

They traveled for the day and into the next, always with one eye on the back trail. They tried following the highway south, but the earthquake damage made for hard going. They were actually happy to move into the hills, as they provided extra concealment.

The second night while they were camped, Morgan brought up a point many of them had already been thinking.

"We're traveling okay if we stick to the hills and mountains. Somehow, like Yellowstone, the earthquake didn't do as much damage. But as we travel on the ridges and I look down to the west, all I see is broken up land. I want to get to the ocean as much as anyone, but I'm beginning to think that it's not going to happen. And based on things Nick and Jason said, I just think it's going to get worse the further south we go."

"I think you're right," said William. "So where does it leave us?"

"I say we head home," said Harry.

"I agree," said Emma. "I'm tired of this."

"We came on this trip to explore," said Wade. "So we can't see the ocean. Who cares? There are plenty of other places to go."

"No, I agree with Harry and Emma," said Morgan. "It's time to go home."

Most of the others nodded in agreement. Darcy was the lone holdout, and Cat knew why. She had nothing to go back to. Her mother didn't want her there and Darcy didn't want to be there.

"Yeah, I think it's time," said Zack with a sigh.

Cat looked at Simon, who gave her an almost imperceptible nod of encouragement, then said, "We're not going back. Wade is right. We came here to explore. I think there are plenty of places east of here to check out. Simon and I are going to continue on."

"And we'll come with you," said Yuki.

"Suit yourselves," said Morgan. "I suggest we stay here tomorrow to rest up. We're low on food, so I'll go hunting. Then those of us who are going home can start back the next day."

It became moot the next afternoon. Morgan came riding back into camp in a hurry without any results from his hunt.

He jumped off his horse while it was still moving and yelled out, "We're definitely being followed. And they're close. We need to move now!"

They were gathering their belongings and saddling their horses almost before Morgan finished speaking. In less than ten minutes they were ready to go. They had just mounted up when they heard the sound of metal scraping against rock.

Morgan turned in the saddle and raised his rifle just as two explosions erupted from the woods. Morgan jerked and then fell to the ground.

There was no doubt in anyone's mind that he was dead.

Chapter 17

Bedlam followed, with most of the teens not sure where to go. Cat and Simon only hesitated a second. They simultaneously pulled out their pistols and fired round after round into the woods, yelling to their friends to get out of there. Neither one of them expected to hit anyone, but they were trying to give the rest of the group time to escape.

As their friends cleared out—with Zack, Wade, and Yuki all following Cat and Simon's lead by shooting into the woods—Simon yelled, "Let's go!" The five remaining teens reached the woods on the other side under a hail of bullets. Miraculously, no one was hit.

They rode steadily for about ten minutes, then stopped to regroup. It was only the five of them. The others were nowhere to be found.

"Did everyone get out?" asked Zack.

"I think so," answered Cat. "I think we need to head east. The country is more open."

"What about the others?" said Zack.

"We can't go looking for them," said Wade. "We have no idea where they are. We just have to hope that they stay safe."

They all looked up when they heard the sound of a horse. In the distance, heading due south, Cat could see a single rider galloping along a trail.

"It's Darcy," said Zack. "I'm going after her. You guys go east. If we can meet up, we will." He took off after Darcy. "Stay safe," he yelled out over his shoulder.

They heard a noise coming from the woods behind them.

"We've gotta get out of here," said Wade. "Let's go."

They rode for hours, seeing none of their group or any of the people following them. When night fell, they found a small hollow to camp for the night. It was well off the trail they had been traveling on. They didn't dare build a fire, and other than a few pieces of jerky, they had nothing to eat. They took turns standing guard.

Yuki was taking her turn on watch while the others tried to sleep, but as tired as they were, sleep wouldn't come.

"Do you think it's the people who killed Clete?" asked Wade.

"It's got to be," answered Simon. "But if so, why are they following us? There has to be a reason behind it. Why would they leave their home—the one they were supposedly protecting by killing Clete—to follow us? It doesn't make sense."

Yuki came in and Wade left to take her place.

"I didn't think you'd be sleeping," she said.

"I'm glad you and Wade are with us," said Cat. "I hope the others are okay."

"I can't believe Morgan is dead," said Yuki. "I didn't like him, and I'm not sure many people did, but nobody deserves to die like that. He saved us. He saved us by warning us about them, and again when he took the first bullets, allowing us to escape. I'll never think of him the same way again." She started to cry, and that brought tears to the eyes of Cat and Simon as well. Eventually, they all fell asleep, Cat and Simon waking up during the night to take their turns at guard duty.

They were up early. There was a heavy mist in the air when they walked their horses out of the hollow and back onto the trail. There was still no sign of their friends, and they could only hope that they were safe.

By mid-afternoon they had reached the end of the mountain range and were standing on a ledge overlooking a vast desert. In the far distance they could see the outline of large peaks and far to the south were faint outlines of rocks, all a reddish-beige color.

"Red Rock country," said Wade. "My mom said she came here as a kid. Said it was beautiful."

"I think we'll still have a better chance going east, but we have the desert in between us and the beautiful country," said Simon, who had been looking over the edge of the ledge. "I suggest we rest here for the night. It looks like a good flat spot under the ledge. Even room for the horses. We can cook some dinner and get a real night's rest."

During the day, Cat had killed a couple of large rabbits with her crossbow. With Simon standing guard in the woods at the top of the ledge, the others prepared the rabbits. They had nothing to go with the meat, but at that point, they didn't care. They just needed to fill their stomachs. Water wasn't a problem, as they had passed numerous lakes and ponds, as well as a few small waterfalls.

While Cat and Yuki cooked, Wade was peering at the map.

"I agree with what Simon said earlier. Our best choice is to cross the desert and try to make it to the mountains on the other side. The map says it was a state called Colorado." He looked up from the map with a worried expression. "We're talking a couple hundred miles across the desert. It could easily take us a week."

"Should we travel at night," asked Cat, "to avoid the heat?"

"Normally, I think that would be best, but with the crevasses, it could get dangerous at night."

"It doesn't look too broken up," said Yuki, shading her eyes against the sun."

"No, it doesn't look like there are any big ones," agreed Wade. "I'm worried about the small cracks, the ones harder to see until you are right on top of them."

"We can do the fastest travel in the early morning and early evening," said Cat, "then take it easy during the worst of the heat. We passed a stream a short way up the trail. We'll need to fill up everything we can with water."

"Do you think they are still chasing us?" asked Yuki.

"We have to go under the assumption that they are," said Wade. "Maybe at some point we'll understand why."

*****

The night passed uneventfully, although none of the teens got any sleep. They filled their canteens, as well as every other bottle they had, in the darkness of the night. They were up a little before sunrise and loaded the horses. It had been decided that they would ride the horses during the cooler hours and walk them in the heat. There was still no sign of their pursuers, but Cat sensed they were behind them.

"Did you see any horses when they attacked us?" she asked suddenly.

The others shook their heads.

"That's why they haven't caught up with us yet. I think they are on foot."

At that moment a shot rang out. The four teens ducked but no bullet hit anywhere close. Then three shots in succession. Again, they saw and heard no bullets.

"It's a signal," said Simon. "Someone has spotted us and is signaling to the rest. We've gotta go."

There was a narrow trail leading from the ledge down to the desert floor far below. It was steep and they had to walk the horses, often sliding a few feet in the process. It took them an hour to reach the bottom. The sun hadn't been up very long and already they were exhausted. If the heat this early in the morning was any indication, Cat knew they were going to be in trouble. But they had nowhere else to go. She looked up to the ledge from where they had started, shading her eyes from the morning sun. People were standing on the ledge looking down on them.

"Look," she said, pointing.

"Oh my God!" exclaimed Yuki.

"How many do you figure?" asked Simon.

"At least thirty," said Wade. "They are all over the place up there."

They heard a shot, then another.

"Hard to be accurate shooting downhill," said Cat, "but they might get one of us by sheer luck. Let's go."

They mounted their horses and took off east across the

desert. When they were well beyond shooting distance, they stopped and looked back. They could make out the forms of many people working their way down the slope.

"No horses," said Simon. "You were right. We have to ride as far as we can before walking the horses."

They rode for two more hours before it became obvious that the horses needed a break. There was no shade anywhere. They put some of their water into a container the horses could drink from and let each horse take a turn. Each of the teens took sips from their canteens, but were well aware of the need to conserve their water.

"Your face is bright red," Simon said to Cat.

"Yours is too. It's not even noon yet, is it?"

"Mid-morning, most likely," said Wade. "We have a lot of hours to go before the sun goes down." He was looking back the way they had come. "Who knows where they are? All I can see are heat waves."

"We have to be at least a couple of hours ahead," said Cat, "and we had the advantage of riding for the last couple of hours, so it's probably more than that. They are on foot, so the heat will slow them down."

"We need to walk, too," said Simon. "The horses need a rest."

"There are some rocks up ahead," said Wade, pointing. "Trouble is, I can't tell if they're two miles or ten. I guess we just keep going and find out."

The heat was unbearable. They tied shirts to their heads to help block out the sun, but it only helped marginally. They had encountered no wide crevasses, but cracks in the ground were everywhere. They had to be aware of where they were walking.

"I wonder what they are doing back home," said Yuki, trying to somehow distract them.

"Probably wondering what we are doing down here," said Simon.

The conversation didn't go much further than that and they lapsed into silence. As it turned out, the rocks Wade had seen were closer to the two-mile mark. They cried out in joy when they approached the rocks, but the joy was short-lived. The whole thing was only fifteen feet high and twenty feet across and provided no shade.

"I still say we rest a while," said Wade.

Cat looked at the sky. "In another hour the sun will be low enough in the sky to give us some shade on this side. We can be out of the sun until it gets cool enough to start off again."

"Do you think we're safe here?" asked Yuki.

"We don't have a whole lot of choice," said Cat. "We all need the rest, including the horses."

They gave the horses some more water, had a few sips themselves, then settled down against the rock. Less than an hour later they found themselves in the shadows. It was still unbearably hot, but at least they were out of the direct sun.

*****

Cat woke up with a start. It was dark. It was cool. She could see the stars overhead. They had overslept!

She looked around in a panic. The others were asleep and the horses were standing quietly off to the side. She shook each of them and whispered, "Get up. We overslept. We need to get going."

They were all wide awake in seconds, each nervously looking back toward the west. Cat climbed into the saddle and waited for the others to get settled before moving off into the night.

It was a cloudless night, allowing them to see the ground fairly well.

"I know we weren't going to travel at night," said Cat, "but it's easy to see tonight, so I think we should keep going. Let's just be extra careful of the ground."

There were no arguments from the others. Fear was driving them, as was the anticipation of traveling in the coolness of the night.

Cat just knew that they had to put a lot of miles between them and their pursuers. How many miles had they lost by sleeping? Were they even still being pursued? The not knowing was almost worse than knowing.

Either way, they just had to keep going.

Chapter 18

With bullets flying all around during the attack, William's horse plunged into the woods on the western side of the clearing with William barely hanging on. He could hear a horse behind him, but was too concerned about falling to look to see who it was.

His horse was spooked and was galloping through the woods, branches slapping at William. He was ducking as low as he could to avoid the branches, while at the same time trying to calm his horse down.

The other horse was still behind him. He snuck a look. It was Harry, and he was also trying to control his horse. They went about a mile before they were able to bring their mounts to a halt. William slid off his horse, while keeping hold of the reins in case the horse got spooked again. Harry stopped next to him and jumped off his horse.

"Oh my God, William! They shot Morgan! Oh my God, oh my God."

"Harry, calm down." William stood up, wiping the dust off himself.

"They shot him right in front of us. I was next to him. That could've been me. What are we going to do?"

"The first thing you're going to do is calm down."

"But what about the others? Are they dead too? What are we going to do?"

William jumped on his brother and threw him to the ground. Harry landed hard and cried out in pain. William stood over him.

"Just shut up for a minute and let me think."

Harry just laid there, not sure whether to be more scared of their attackers or of his brother.

"We've gotta go back and try to help," said William.

"We can't go back. They'll kill us."

"You just want to leave your friends? Do you think they'd leave you?"

"But we don't even know where they are. William, let's just go home. They can send people out to help them."

"Even if we go all out and make good time, it might take us a week to get home, and then another week for them to get here. It'll be two or three weeks before they could help. By then it'll be too late. I'm going back. You want to come or not?"

Harry was on the verge of crying. "Okay, I'll come, but ... but just let me clean up." He burst into tears. "I crapped my pants."

William, a little softer now, said, "Go ahead. I'll wait."

Harry pulled some clean underwear and some toilet paper from his saddlebag and went into the woods. William tightened the cinch on his saddle and on his brother's. He bent down to pick up his pistol, which had fallen out of his holster, when something huge landed on him, knocking him to the ground.

"Where are they?" came a deep voice from on top of him. The smell was enough to make William's eyes water.

"There's another horse," came another voice. "Someone else is here."

"You gonna tell me?" the man said, two inches from William's ear.

"No one. No one but me." William had never been so scared.

The man heaved William to his feet and punched him in the face. William went down hard, landing awkwardly on his arm. He screamed in pain.

"One last time. Who else is here? You don't answer, I kill you. Simple."

The pain was making him dizzy. He was sure he was going to pass out. Where was Harry?

His silent question was answered when he heard the second man yell out, "Found him. The kid shit his…"

An explosion ripped through the air and William heard the other man hit the ground with a thud.

"What the…" The man holding William let go and turned toward the woods where Harry had gone in. William looked up to see his brother emerge from the woods awkwardly, his pants down to his ankles. He was holding his pistol with both hands and it was pointed at the man next to William. Harry's hands were shaking badly.

"Get away from my brother."

The man took a step toward Harry and Harry pulled the trigger. The bullet hit the tree next to the man. He pulled the trigger again. This time the bullet hit the man in the chest. He went down soundlessly. Harry approached him and pointed his gun at the man on the ground, who was now groaning. He shot three more bullets into the man and then dropped the gun. He stood there silently.

"Harry, we've got to go." The pain was tremendous. William looked down at his arm. There was no doubt it was broken. They had to get away from there.

"Harry!"

Harry looked up at him, his eyes vacant.

"Harry, you've got to help me get on my horse. Pull up your pants."

Hi brother didn't move.

"Now!"

Wordlessly, Harry pulled up his jeans, leaving his gun sitting in the dirt. He moved robotically to his brother and helped him into his saddle.

"Now pick up your gun and get on your horse. We're going home."

At the sound of those words, Harry mounted his horse, still leaving his gun in the dirt.

*****

They rode day and night. William tied himself to his saddle as best he could with one hand. His brother was lost in his own world and William was afraid that if he fell off the horse, Harry would never notice.

William led the way until they reached a familiar part of the trail and Harry knew where they were. Silently, he led the way, going as fast as they could and only resting when the horses were about to collapse. When they stopped for the night, they had jerky and water. William would take that time to readjust and tighten the splint he'd put on the broken arm. The pain was worse than anything he had ever experienced.

During one of the stops, he stumbled over a rock and landed on his arm. He passed out. When he woke up an hour later, he could see the bone. He covered it the best he could with a bandage and then resplinted it.

Almost a week after they started, they rode into the town of Rock Creek, William slumped in his saddle, delirious with pain and fever, and Harry still staring vacantly straight ahead, having not said a single word the whole trip back.

Chapter 19

Four weeks had passed and Ben and Lila were not coping as well as they hoped with Cat suddenly out of their life. They thought they had prepared themselves for her eventual departure, but in fact, they were finding it emotionally difficult. They were going through the motions in just about all of their chores.

They weren't alone. In her daily journeys to town, Lila ran across other parents having a similarly hard time. The general mood in Yellowstone was melancholy. Four weeks and things weren't any better. Even those without children were feeling the mood.

Ben and Lila had just wrapped up their chores for the day and were talking about getting away for a few days when they heard a horse gallop into the yard. They rushed to the door. It was Sean.

"Get into town," he called from the saddle. "Two of the boys have returned, and they are in bad shape. They're at the doc's now."

He waited while Ben and Lila saddled their horses.

"It's William and Harry. They were almost dead when they

arrived. William has a severely broken arm and a broken collarbone and is in and out of consciousness, and Harry is out of his mind with fear. I couldn't get anything out of them. The other parents are all being told. Most will probably be there when we return."

A large crowd had gathered outside the doctor's office. The only people allowed in were William and Harry's parents. Ben knew all the other parents had the same thoughts he was having: what had happened to the rest of the group?

It was hours before they heard anything. It was well into the evening and the crowd had only grown larger. Brittany and Sean brought a large pot of stew and pitchers of water. Despite their worry, people were hungry and appreciated the food.

Finally, about five hours after arriving for the vigil, William and Harry's parents emerged from the office. As they came out, the doctor quietly called Morgan's parents into the office. William and Harry's parents were met with a million questions and the father held up his hand for silence.

"I know you are all worried about your kids, and I'm sorry it's taken so long, but Harry finally started talking just a little while ago."

"How are your boys?" asked Lila.

"Thanks for asking. I know you are all worried about your own. Harry is okay physically, but I think it will be a long road emotionally. William is still unconscious. The doctor says he will live, but it's touch and go as to whether he will lose his arm. The bone came through the skin and it is badly infected. The doc is doing all he can." His voice choked as he said it. "As for the rest of the group, Harry doesn't know where they are. They were attacked and they all scattered. Morgan got hit and

Harry thinks he died."

A gasp went up in the group and tears began to flow. He then related the story Harry had told him about being followed and eventually attacked.

"Harry said the consensus of the group was that it was probably the same people who killed Clete. When they got attacked, the bullets were flying everywhere and the kids were all lucky to get out of there. He doesn't know where the rest of them are. He said it was hard going and they had all decided to turn eastward when they were attacked. He can show us on a map about where it all happened."

"How long ago? asked Aaron.

"At least a week."

"Holy shit," said someone in the crowd. "They could be anywhere by now."

"We've got to try," said Lila. "I suggest those of us who are going meet tomorrow and head out as quickly as we can. Those who are staying should be heavily armed, just in case. The whole community should be on constant alert.

"We shouldn't have let her go," said Ben on the way home. "She's too young."

"Ben, how old were we when we were left on our own?"

"That was different. We didn't have a choice."

"We also didn't have any skills. We survived as much out of luck as we did from the things we learned. Cat is so much more prepared than we were. She's totally in tune with her surroundings, she's an excellent shot with a rifle, a pistol, and a crossbow, and she can live off the land."

"You're right."

"And here's the other thing. The world we entered was

explosive. People didn't trust each other and there was violence everywhere we turned. Not anymore. It's been seventeen years. Things have settled down. This one group is a throwback to the old days, unfortunately. We don't know their motives or anything about them. I'm just as concerned as you are, but there is nothing we can do about what has happened. We can only find out if she's okay. But if there are any two people who can take care of themselves, it's Cat and Simon."

"You're right. It'll do no good to worry. But if anything at all has happened to Cat, those people are going to feel my wrath."

"Our wrath, and they won't know what hit them."

*****

They met the next morning at dawn in the center of town. Ben and Lila were joined by Aaron, Sean, Nick, Jason, and an assortment of the parents of the other kids, and a few others who just wanted to help. There were twenty grim-faced rescuers in all. Each carried a heavy load of weapons and ammunition. They also brought dried and smoked food, as they would have no time to stop and hunt. They wanted to reach the ambush spot in half the time it took their kids. They expected some hard riding and each trailed a second horse behind so that they always had a fresh mount.

There was no time for goodbyes. Harry had given them a general idea of the route, and they started the rescue mission at a full gallop. The first night they didn't stop until well after dark, eating their dried food and building a small fire for coffee. They allowed themselves only a few hours of sleep and were on their way before daybreak, when there was just enough light to see by.

Their route took them through Jackson, and then west to Lava Hot Springs, where they turned south toward Salt Lake City. They had picked up the teens' trail the first day and found it fairly easy to follow. Most of the parents in the group knew their own child's horse's hoofprints. With the long riding days and the ability to follow the kids' trail, they were on the road to Salt Lake City in days, as opposed to the two weeks it took the teens.

They didn't expect to run across the attackers until at least Salt Lake City, which is why they were surprised to hear gunfire as they were passing Logan.

Aaron heard it first.

"Firefight east of here."

They were skirting the western edge of Logan. It meant the fighting was coming from the hills to the east of town.

The others stopped and listened. There was an intense battle going on.

"A lot of firepower," said Sean, pulling out his M-16. "We'll get close enough to try to get a feel for what's going on, then we'll make our plan from there."

Serving as active-duty Marines when the event happened, most people listened to Sean and Aaron when it came to tactical matters.

They galloped through the dead town of Logan and into the hills beyond, getting closer to the gunfire. When he felt they were close enough, Sean put up his hand and they all jumped off their horses and tied them to low tree branches. They made their way through the trees to some rocks overlooking a wide canyon.

It only took a minute to grasp the situation. There was a group on the canyon floor hiding behind whatever cover they could find. Luckily for them, there were trees and a number of large rocks. It wasn't their children. Doing a quick count, Ben figured there had to be a couple dozen people down there. Some of them were shooting, but most were just trying to stay hidden. Also hidden behind rocks were some vehicles. They looked like small tractors with extra-large wheels. There was a story there, he thought. When he looked into the hills overlooking the canyon, Ben knew they had found their quarry. He could see lots of men dressed in shabby clothes. Most of them had beards, and many of the beards were gray.

"They're the ones who killed Clete and set the fire at Yellowstone. They're the ones we're looking for."

"They are all scattered on the side of the hills. If we can get above them," said Aaron, "we can shoot down on them and catch them totally exposed. Half of you come with me and we'll take the hill on the right. The other half go with Sean to the left side. When we are all in position, we'll take them out."

With no objections, they all started on their way, Ben and Lila following Aaron to the right side of the canyon. It didn't take long for them to reach their destination. As they ran along the crest of the hill, Aaron suddenly stopped and motioned for the others to drop down on the ground.

"There's one on top. If we go any further, he'll see us and warn the rest before we get into position."

"Leave him to me," said Ben. He left his rifle and crawled along the top with his crossbow. The man was shooting down into the canyon and hadn't yet noticed Ben. Ben got to within thirty feet of the shooter before bringing up his crossbow, aiming, and shooting. The man went down silently as the arrow penetrated his brain.

"I still have trouble believing you are the same wimpy little brother I knew way back when," said Aaron, when he caught up to Ben. He handed Ben his rifle, then said to them all, "let's spread out. Pick your targets on the other hill, then when I tell you, start shooting."

In five minutes everyone was in place. Aaron and Sean must have had their own signal, because suddenly Ben heard Aaron shout, "Let's do it!"

Bullets rained down and the men on the hillside had little cover from above and scrambled to find any shelter from the attack. Seeing that help had arrived, the people in the valley came out from hiding and started firing into the hills, as well. Getting hit from every direction proved too much for the men on the hillside and the fighting was over in less than twenty minutes. Everyone on the hillside was either dead, wounded, or in the case of a very few individuals left standing, holding their hands up in surrender. When the fighting was over, those on the canyon floor came to greet the people who had saved their lives.

There were only four prisoners. Sean and some of the others took them and tied them up in a little grove of trees. Meanwhile, Ben, Lila, and the rest of the group went to greet those who had been under attack.

"Thank you for coming when you did," said an older man with a strong Scottish accent. "I didn't know how we were going to survive this." At least that was what Ben thought he said. He had never heard such a thick accent before.

Another man approached. He was a little younger than the first man and spoke with an American accent.

"I wondered if I would ever see you again. The rumors were you were dead, but I didn't believe them."

"Holy crap," said Ben, suddenly recognizing the man. "Dan!"

Chapter 20

The years fell away in Ben's memory. Standing before him was an older version—maybe close to sixty now—of a man who had meant a lot to Ben and Lila on their trip south after the event.

He gave Dan a hug, and then got out of the way so that Lila could hug him as well.

Dan held Lila away from him and looked her over.

"My God, you turned into a beautiful woman. I like the eye patch. Are you going for the pirate look? Makes you look mysterious."

Leave it to Dan, thought Ben, to approach the subject of Lila's eye patch directly and not give her the opportunity to feel self-conscious about it around an old friend.

Ben turned to his brother. "Aaron, this is Dan. Dan, my brother, Aaron."

"The brother in California you thought was dead?"

"Imagine my surprise."

Ben addressed his group. "Lila and I met Dan not long into our trip south. He and his friend Gordon, and Gordon's wife, ended up prisoners in the same camp with Lila, and then I saw them later when I was kidnapped to help rebuild DC." He looked at Dan. "I heard about Gordon. I'm sorry."

"God, I haven't thought about Gordon in years. Yes, it was sad. He just never recovered from the death of his wife. I'm happy though to hear that the rumors of your deaths were greatly exaggerated. What are you doing out here?"

Ben gave Dan a condensed version of their life over the last sixteen years, ending with their current mission to find Cat and her friends.

"I would offer to help, but these people need me to guide them and I'm afraid we would just slow you down."

"So what exactly are you doing here?" asked Lila.

"It's a long story. It's getting dark. Would you join us for the night and I can tell you all about it?"

With most of the attackers dead and the rest prisoners, they decided that the kids wouldn't be in anymore harm if they stopped early for the night.

"What do we do about the prisoners?" one of the parents asked Aaron. "They are refusing to talk."

"Keep them bound. Don't feed them and don't go near them. We'll let them sweat it out for a while. They'll eventually talk. I guarantee it."

*****

Dinner was provided by Dan's group, which numbered twenty-four, many with heavy accents. They had hunted the day before with great success, and were happy to share their bounty with their rescuers. As they ate, Dan gave his story.

"First of all, I'd like to introduce Angus McPherson. He

and his group, as if you couldn't tell, are from Scotland. I'll get to their story in a minute."

Angus took a moment to once more thank Ben and his group for coming in the nick of time. Again, Ben had trouble understanding him, so Angus really could have been saying anything.

"Things didn't go well in DC," began Dan. "They did at first, once Colonel Jeffries took over as president. He was determined to get the country going again. He was a good man and for the first year or so a lot of progress was made. We tried to get the word out that the government was still functioning and slowly people made their way to Washington. At one point we had almost a thousand residents, if you include the soldiers who had already been there. Jeffries liked me and made me a part of the administration."

His face took on a sad expression. "Unfortunately, the universe had other plans. About a year after he took over, Jeffries died. He developed a bad case of pneumonia and just didn't recover."

"That wasn't the plague we heard about, was it?" asked Nick.

"No, that came later. For some reason, I was asked to take over as president. Don't ask me why."

"No need to be modest," said Lila. "I bet you did a great job."

"We'll never know. That plague you mentioned happened after I'd been in the job about a year. A man showed up in Washington one day, delirious and with a high fever. He said that communities north of Washington were being devastated by a plague. So of course, the idiot, who was obviously infected, brought it to us. The city was wiped out in days. And some of our people left and probably infected other areas."

He sighed. "Well, the writing was on the wall and the only thing left to do was leave town. There were about a half dozen of us who hadn't yet been infected. We left individually and promised to meet at a spot on the Potomac in a week. Anyone still alive by then wasn't going to catch it—everyone who picked up the bug died within seventy-two hours. After a week, the six of us met up. We hadn't lost anyone. We decided to leave the country and see if the rest of the world was in as bad shape as America. I'm a good sailor—had been sailing all my life—and there were all of these beautiful sailboats moored on the Potomac. We just had to find one that was big enough to make a transatlantic journey, but one that wasn't completely reliant on computers—which, of course, were useless. It took a few days, but we found one. We loaded it with supplies and started on our way."

He looked at Ben. "Someone you know was with us. When you left Washington, do you remember running across a middle-aged black man and his young daughter? He said you saved him from getting hanged by three racist assholes."

"I do remember. He seemed to be a college professor-type and I directed him to Washington."

"He came with his daughter, and I ended up working with him. He and his daughter survived and made the sea journey with us. They stayed in Scotland and are very happy. You never know what effects a good deed might have on another person. He told me when I left to thank you if I ever ran across you."

Ben was pleased. His gut feeling had told him that the man

was one of the good ones. He was happy to know that he hadn't been wrong.

"Anyway, it was a rough crossing at times, with storms blowing in constantly, but we made it to Europe. After days of travelling the coast of Great Britain—which fared no better than America from the event—we ended up in Scotland, where I met Angus."

He motioned toward his Scottish friend, and in dramatic fashion announced, "Angus here, is almost single-handedly providing the world with power."

Chapter 21

Ben and the others let Dan's comment sink in.

"Okay, you have our attention," said Jason.

"Sorry," said Dan, grinning. "I wanted to say it with a flourish, but the fact is, Angus can help us rebuild the world."

"You are being dramatic again," said Lila, with a smile.

"I guess I am. But it's true. Angus is—was—the chief engineer of a massive combination solar and wind farm company on the coast of Scotland. Angus was under the water inspecting some of the wind turbine bases when the catastrophe hit. Many of the others in his company were in their underground offices. In fact, the group you see here are only a third of the employees that survived. The rest are still in Scotland, running the facility."

"Weren't the circuits fried in all of the wind turbines and solar panels?" asked Nick.

"They were, but most of the company is located below ground, including the manufacturing and storage facilities. They chose to do it that way to allow for more space for the solar panels above ground. Also, that part of coastal Scotland doesn't have the most hospitable weather. It just made it easier for everyone. Anyway, because everything was below ground, they had replacement circuit boards for everything and—best of all—the capability to manufacture more. Within months…"

"Within weeks," corrected Angus.

"Within weeks, they were up and running to almost full capacity. Over the years, they have supplied much of Great Britain with the tools to regain power, and have expanded into France and Germany."

"How have you been able to get the materials to manufacture enough of them?" asked Lila.

"We already had them," answered Angus in his thick brogue.

"You have to understand," said Dan, knowing that Angus's explanation would be lost if he spoke more than a couple of sentences, "Angus's company supplied wind and solar power units to countries and large corporations. Their own wind and solar farm also provided power to the local region. They had—and still have—large supplies of premade solar units, as well as the materials to make many more. What they are supplying to their own and neighboring countries is a drop in the bucket compared to what they used to ship out every week. Their supply isn't endless, but it's close to it."

"And you're here to share?" asked Sean.

"Exactly. Britain and parts of Europe have a good start. There are whole towns now that are running on solar or wind power. Angus and his people have even adapted solar power onto vehicles, as you will see. We brought a few with us. They look like oversized riding mowers. They fit them with large balloon tires to make it over the rocky terrain. So we loaded up as many solar units as possible onto a ship and headed to America. We found deep tributaries off the California coast, some that extended hundreds of miles inland, so we followed them in."

"The California coast still exists?"

"In places. California didn't fall completely into the ocean, but it may as well have. It's pretty unlivable."

Nick was puzzled. "You came from Scotland, but ended up on the western side of the U.S.? How did that happen?"

"America was meant to be the last stop on the journey. We've been gone almost eight months. The ship dropped us off on this coast and is going to meet us on the east coast, sailing around the tip of South America. We have some seasoned sailors running the ship. We have enough units and parts to leave with quite a few communities—assuming there are some."

"There are," said Ben. "We can give you a pretty accurate map of the locations of many of them. I should warn you that in the middle of the country in particular, there are quite a few crevasses."

"We're prepared. Remember, I lived here too. I had to deal with them back east. We have a lightweight portable bridge."

"You're not walking, right?"

"No, like you, we travel by horseback. That's how most people travel in Europe. We brought horses with us on the ship. One question: I was surprised to run across this bunch. Is there still a lot of violence here?"

"No. We were also surprised. We ran across them a ways back. I'm anxious to find out who they are. But no, I can't see you running across any other trouble. That died out years ago."

"As it did in Europe. It was bad for a while, but slowly civilization caught up with them."

"How has it been in some of the other countries you visited on your way here?" asked Lila.

"We didn't venture inland too far from the coast in most of them. Unless we had someone on the ship who was familiar with the country, we stayed on the coast. Spain, Greece, and Italy had small pockets of people. The African countries the same. South Africa was surprisingly well populated—by that I mean a few thousand. On the opposite side of the spectrum was Japan. We didn't find one soul. Not one. Doesn't mean they weren't there. We just didn't find any."

He continued. "Anyway, we'll make Yellowstone our first stop and leave you with a couple of solar units and a tractor. The solar units are connected to generators. We'll also leave instructions on how to build simple, but effective windmills and leave you with materials to build electrical circuitry."

"Given the working parts, Aaron and I can do that," said Sean. "That was our specialty in the Marines."

"Good. Hopefully our instructions are simple enough so that people in other communities who don't have the background you have can build them. Many of the larger parts needed can be scavenged from cities and towns. We will drop our units off at as many communities as possible before we run out."

Aaron looked at Ben. "Paradise?"

"Dan," said Ben. "Could you leave us enough for another small town? I'd like to take it to them myself. I kind of owe them."

"Done. I'm hoping that by leaving all of this with certain

communities, America can slowly get some of its power back and build from there. The power will help with so many things."

"We've kind of gotten used to life without electricity," said Ben.

"Not much will change for a long time, but slowly you will come to appreciate some of the benefits of having power again."

Lila looked at Angus. "Thank you for doing this. You could have sat on it yourself, and there are many who would have, but you've chosen to share it with the rest of the world. It's very generous."

"It's what humanity is all about," said Angus.

Chapter 22

It was time to check on the prisoners. As much as he was enjoying his talk with Dan, Ben was anxious to learn about Cat and her friends. He, Aaron, and Sean walked into the woods to the clearing where the men were being guarded by Wade and Simon's fathers.

"They haven's said a word, not even to each other," Wade's father said quietly. "Don't get too close to them. They stink."

Ben nodded and approached the prisoners. The man wasn't kidding. The odor was enough to make him vomit. He breathed shallowly, hoping it would help with the smell. The men were filthy and their clothes were even worse. They were barefoot and had strangely misshapen feet. He was getting dizzy from the smell. He'd have to make this fast.

"You will talk," he announced. "There is no way you are leaving here without talking to us."

One of the men gave a snort, then went silent. Ben went over to him and kicked him in the side. The man cried out and fell over.

"Anyone else want to laugh?"

"Ben." Aaron was at his side. "Let's talk." He pulled Ben away and out of the clearing.

Ben was seething. "I can make them talk. I have to. Cat's life is at stake."

"It'll be dark soon. There's nothing we can do tonight to help Cat. We know she got away. You just have to trust that she made it somewhere safely. These guys will talk. Let's just give them a little time. We're not feeding them—and they can smell the food—and we're not giving them water. It's just a matter of time. Go talk some more with your friend."

Ben knew his brother was right, so he walked back to the group and sat down next to Lila. She looked him questioningly. He shook his head and mouthed the words, "not yet."

Someone had just asked Dan to describe the world they'd seen in a little more detail.

"Angus's people had traveled by land through France, Belgium, and into Germany early on. Things were bad."

"Worse than bad," said Angus. "We lost a few people."

"They had sent people out to find clusters of survivors, not so much to set them up with power, but just to find out how bad it was out there. Angus had about eighty people in his group, almost all of them fellow workers. Angus was chosen to be the one in charge, partly because he was the highest one in the company to have survived, and partly because people trusted him. And having spent a lot of years with him, it's no wonder. He's a natural leader. Anyway, two of the scouts never came back. The group he sent out to find them discovered their bodies, but also discovered the people who killed them. It was a vicious group, and his people just barely made it back. They let several years pass before they tried it again. By then I had arrived and I volunteered to go out."

He took a sip of coffee. "What I found was peace. As in America, things had settled down and the few survivors left had formed communities, just like here. We found seventeen communities across Great Britain, France, and Germany. Now we know of nearly a hundred more. We spent a few years getting the equipment to the towns, and as I said before, a lot of that part of Europe now has power. People have been good about sharing. I think we've all realized that the only way we're going to survive is by cooperation. Once we felt we had gone far enough by land, we decided to take to the sea. Angus's company had a massive ship, and they spent a year converting it to solar power. We took off with what we hoped would be enough equipment to get several countries started. The sad part is that we have more equipment left than we thought we would by this time."

"And the rest of the world?" asked Ben.

"Depends where you are. We found two small communities in Northern Ireland, and one in Ireland. In both cases, they knew of no other groups. We went down the coast to Spain and Portugal—a little more life—and then through the Straits of Gibraltar to Italy, Greece, Turkey, Israel, and some of the African countries. We encountered people in all of the countries in various stages of survival. There were fewer people in the Northern African and Middle-Eastern countries. We were told that famine killed many of those who had survived the initial event."

Nobody talked. It was fascinating for them all to hear what was going on in the rest of the world. Assumptions and wonderings were put to rest.

"We then came back out past Gibraltar—which, by the way, had a thriving community of more than sixty people—then down the African coast. There were a lot of the countries we avoided, mostly because we couldn't find a clear path to dock. Sometimes it was questionable shoals, and sometimes the harbors were just filled with too many derelict ships for us to enter. As I said before, South Africa was doing very well and we rid ourselves of quite a number of the units. I think as the years pass, South Africa will become one of the leading countries in the world—if we ever get that far. We then went part way up the eastern coast of Africa before heading across to India. Yes, there were a lot of countries we missed, but we couldn't do them all. And frankly, after South Africa, we weren't finding an awful lot of people."

"How about India?"

"You would think that India, with the population it had, would be thriving. Nothing. We didn't find one soul. We also had a rule that we wouldn't venture far into the country. If we didn't find people in a few days, we moved on. Malaysia, Indonesia, the Philippines, and even Taiwan all had communities, but not many. The scariest part of our trip was when we hit Japan. I mentioned before that it was devoid of people, but what I didn't say was how spooky it was. A number of our people said they had visions of dead people calling out to them. It wasn't like anything we had ever seen or experienced. We couldn't wait to leave."

He took a breath. "Then we came here. We maneuvered in as far as we could and we started on our way by horseback. It was exciting for me to be back here, and I think it was exciting for many of the others because they had heard so much about the States. And so here we are."

"I think you will be happy with what you find," said Lila. "After a rough start—one that you remember well, I'm sure—things have settled down nicely. There are a lot of good people out there. Other than this crew—and we still don't know anything about them—we haven't heard of any violence in many years."

Ben stood up. "Speaking of this crew, now let's go see what those men have to say. And I'm in no mood to have them stay silent."

Chapter 23

Darkness settled in, and Ben, Aaron, and Sean used the opportunity to observe the four prisoners without being seen. The prisoners were in front of the fire, which was blinding them to anything else. None of the prisoners had spoken, either to their captors or to each other.

"What do you think?" asked Ben.

"Let's see what you've picked up over the years, little brother," said Aaron. "What do you see?"

"God, always the big brother," said Ben, rolling his eyes. "Okay, I see three of them staring directly into the fire. They are sullen. Their eyes are vacant. I think we could talk to them until we turn blue in the face and would get nothing out of them. Even if they talked, I don't think they'd have much of anything to say that would be helpful. The fourth guy is different. He's looking around. He's trying not to stare into the fire. He probably suspects that we are watching him, but he can't do anything about it. He's older than the others and looks like he's more intelligent—which isn't saying much. I say we go after him."

"Let's do it," said Aaron. He called Nick and Jason over

and asked them to take away the other three. When they were gone, Ben, Aaron, and Sean entered the circle of light and sat facing the man. To be fair to him, they sat off to the side of the fire rather than in front of it, so he could view his interrogators.

He watched them with a combination of fear and curiosity. Nothing they did escaped his eyes. When they first approached him, he drew back in fear. The kept their distance. The smell emanating from him was overpowering. Sean likened it to a combination of rotting fish and rancid meat.

From a safe smelling distance of twenty feet, Ben watched him. He was older than most of the rest he'd seen—maybe his early sixties—and unlike some of the dead ones they had examined, he had most of his teeth, a fact that would help if they could ever get him to talk. His shaggy, gray hair extended past his shoulder blades, and his beard lay flat on his chest. There were signs that he had cut both his beard and his hair at various points in the past, as the ends were squared off in places, but ragged nonetheless. He wore ill-fitting glasses that were scratched and cracked. He was barefoot, and his misshapen feet had inch-deep callouses. Ben figured that he hadn't worn shoes in many years. His clothes were ill-fitting as well, probably taken off one of his group who had died long ago. With the number of holes and rips Ben observed, it wouldn't be long before the clothes fell off him altogether. One of the dead ones had been wearing newer clothes, probably once belonging to Clete.

"Now that we are facing him, what do you think?" Sean whispered to Ben.

"Other than his group, I don't think he's seen another soul in seventeen years. He looks at us as if he can't believe he's looking at other humans. Up until now, as a group, they haven't traveled far from their home in the mountains. If they had, they wouldn't look like that. They would have raided stores for clothes and boots and glasses."

"They have guns and ammo."

"That's one of the answers we have to try to pry out of him."

They tried for fifteen minutes, utilizing every strategy, from intimidation to friendship.

He stared at the ground.

"Well, I'm done for now," said Aaron, getting up. "I've had enough of the stench."

"I'm trying to get used to it so I can get closer to him to talk without throwing up," said Ben.

"You're a better man than I … or just plain stupid." He got up, with Sean following, leaving Ben sitting there alone.

Ben looked at the prisoner and decided to give it one more try.

"Do you have any idea how badly you stink?"

No response.

"That's why nobody wants to be near you. When was the last time you took a bath?"

No response.

Ben sighed.

"So here's what I think, and correct me if I'm wrong. You haven't seen anyone else since the event that killed almost everyone on the planet." The man cocked his head to the side ever so slightly. "So up until the time you killed the young man near your home, you didn't even know any other humans existed. Did you think you were the only people left on earth?"

The man looked directly at him. Ben saw that as progress.

"Did you think we were aliens or something?"

"Some did."

He spoke!

"I suppose I can understand that. It tells me that you have no idea what happened. Would you like me to tell you?"

"How do you know?" It was said with a mixture of sullenness and fear. He wanted to know, but he didn't want to trust Ben.

"Because I was there when the man who caused all of this died. It was our own president, the President of the United States." The man opened his eyes wide. "If he hadn't died on his own, I would have killed him."

Ben proceeded to tell the man a shortened version of the story of his journey south with Lila so many years before, and how he was "drafted" by the president to help rebuild Washington, in the process hearing the story of how the president was responsible for setting off a powerful nuclear weapon that had had unexpected and devastating results. Just telling the story brought Ben back to those early days and how long ago it now seemed.

"Our own president?"

Ben nodded. "I know he didn't plan for this to happen, but his own greed and desire for power caused it. As a result, there are very few people left alive. There are a few dozen communities across the country with survivors. It was hard at first, and there was a lot of distrust and violence, but over time things settled down. Now most of the communities are thriving and people are trying to build the country again."

"The rest of the world?" Ben knew that he had him now.

His curiosity had overcome his fear.

"The same. Those people we stopped you from killing were from Europe. They had come over here to see what had happened to America. Until they came, we had no idea what had happened to the rest of the world. If you had killed them, we'd still never know. Now we know that they suffered the same fate as us. Like us, they are trying to rebuild. They actually have a source for electricity, something we don't have here." As he said it, Ben had pangs of guilt, thinking about what he had done in Paradise.

"Look," he continued. "I understand that this must all be a shock to you, seeing other people. You're scared. I get that. You've become someone you probably weren't seventeen years ago."

"It's been that long?"

"Yes. And in seventeen years, I've seen everything. I've seen people help each other and I've seen people kill each other. We've all been afraid. None of us knew what happened. As a result, a lot of bad things happened between people. But that's over now. No one is judging you. But you have to understand that we have ten of our children out there and we don't know where they are. We want to find them. You've got to talk to me. We're not going to kill you and we're not going to hurt you."

"I want you to."

"To what?"

"Kill me. I'm tired. I just want to die. Many times I've thought about jumping off a cliff or shooting myself, but I never did. I'm tired of living like this."

"Did you have children back when all this happened?"

asked Ben gently.

He nodded and tears filled his eyes.

"And grandchildren. So long ago. They died I guess. They didn't live nearby. Two daughters and two new babies I had never seen. My wife was dead when I got back to the house. Peaceful, like she just went to sleep."

"Please tell me your story."

The man looked at him and sighed. Ben wasn't exactly sure what the sigh indicated—hurt? Despair?—but he knew the man was ready to talk.

*****

"We're all miners," the man began. "Or, we were. We worked at a big silver mine. There were 120 of us underground when it happened. Suddenly, the lights went out. That's how we knew something had happened. But we weren't worried. The lights went out on a regular basis. We just waited for the backup system to kick in, but it never did. We tried radioing the top to find out what was happening, but nobody answered. We had our flashlights and other portable lamps and we knew where everyone was working. It took a few hours, but eventually we were all accounted for and we started making our way to the top. Unlike some mines, we didn't have to rely on an elevator. There was a road. There would usually have been one of the transport vehicles to take us up, but both of them were up top. So we walked."

It was bringing back some painful memories, so Ben didn't hurry him.

"We made it to the top and that's when we found everyone

dead—all of our co-workers and all of our families. It was a terrible day. There was no sign of how they died, so everyone had a theory. It was the Russians; it was the Chinese; it was the North Koreans; it was a gas leak, sun spots, chemical spill; you name it. The radios we had with us underground still worked, but nothing up top worked. We tried to contact people, but nobody answered. We talked about traveling out of the valley and finding someone alive to help us, or at least provide some information. It was soon after that that an earthquake hit. It collapsed the mine and destroyed the road to the nearest town. It took us a couple of days to walk the ten miles. When we arrived, we found the whole town destroyed and everyone dead."

Now that he was talking, the story poured out.

"We were scared before, but now we were terrified. We searched through the wreckage and took everything we could find, including clothes and food. There was a gun store, so we cleaned it out. We were facing an enemy, but we didn't know who it was. We had to be ready for anything." He made a face. "That's when one of the guys came up with the alien theory. It was stupid, but a lot of the guys believed it. They said it was the only explanation for why we hadn't seen any planes and why the military hadn't come to help."

As much as Ben hated the man for what they did to Clete and for attacking the Europeans, he was beginning to feel sorry for him.

"Whether it was aliens or the Russians, we knew we hadn't been discovered, so we decided it would be best for us to stay where we were, rather than to leave and risk getting caught and killed or tortured, or be tested on by the aliens."

Ben looked at him incredulously.

"Hey, you've gotta understand. We were just a bunch of miners. Most of us had been doing it our whole lives. The only people with any kind of education were the bosses, and they were all up top when it happened. I had two years of college, which made me one of the smarter ones down there. What does that tell you? Anyway," he continued, "we stayed all this time. We never left, except once. People were missing alcohol, and then someone remembered that Butte City wasn't too many miles away and they had a bar of sorts, so a bunch of them went. I thought it was stupid to risk everything for alcohol, but they did it anyway. They came back with cases of whiskey and other stuff. They carried it by hand over the mountain. Stupid. But it didn't stop me from getting drunk with the others. We stayed drunk for days."

He looked at the ground. When he looked up, he actually had tears in his eyes.

"That was the beginning of the end for the women."

Chapter 24

Ben looked up in surprise. "What women?"

The man shook his head sadly.

"Three of the miners were women. It's not a business that attracts a lot of women, but they were as good as any of the men down there. Anyway, you get over a hundred men and three women, and then you add a lot of whiskey, and what do you think you get? Those women didn't stand a chance ... not a fucking chance. They were nice, too. They didn't deserve it. They got passed around like ... well, you get the idea."

"What happened?"

"One killed herself. She just couldn't take it. I don't blame her. Another was beaten to death by one of the guys when she put up a fight. He was immediately killed by some of the others for doing that. The third? Well, she lasted a while, then just kinda wore out. Someone found her dead one morning. She just died."

Ben couldn't say anything. It brought him back to the early days after the event and some of the atrocities that he and Lila had seen.

Finally he said, "So what made you leave your valley after

seventeen years?"

"I guess the chance to find women. By then, there were only fifty-eight of us left. Over the years, guys died of lots of different things—pneumonia, probably cancer, accidents, and fights. As a group we had become not much more than animals. It was pretty bad. I'd wanted to kill myself for a while, but just didn't. Anyway, some of the guys were out hunting one day when they ran across that boy from your group. You've gotta understand, we hadn't seen another human in all those years and a lot of the guys still thought aliens were out there somewhere. When they found your boy, the first thing they did was to take off a finger to see if he bled like a human. That's when he told them about your town in Yellowstone. After all those years, they finally stopped believing it was aliens."

"Did you set the fire?"

"Not me. I didn't want nothing to do with it. I stayed back in the valley. Your boy told them that there were a lot of women there. He also told us that there were a couple of thousand people living there. So they thought if they started a fire, it would drive you people out and they could pluck the women out when everyone ran. Then they'd bring them back to the valley. Stupid plan, but after all those years, the idea of having women was just too much for them to pass up. It didn't work out. I'm told the fire changed direction and came back quickly. We lost one of our people. They came back to the valley and eventually we all decided it was time to leave, now that we knew there were other people out there. Even I was ready to leave by then. The plan was to watch you people and steal some of the women and try to find a new place to live."

"Why did you torture him and cut him to pieces?"

"Not me. I wasn't there. I don't know why they did it, other than to make sure no one came to our valley. I told you that by now we aren't much more than animals. We've gone crazy, the whole lot of us, me included. The best thing that can happen is you kill us all. Those other three you got, by the way, you'd be best to kill them now. They're the worst of the bunch. They were the worst even when we were human."

"How do you get around?" Ben asked.

"We walk." The man lifted a disgusting foot to show Ben the callouses. "We can go as fast as any horses over this broken ground. Anyway, we were coming back to Yellowstone when we saw all those kids leaving. There were five girls in the group. Young girls. That was too much for my people ... " He stopped for a moment. "... even for me, to resist. So we followed them."

"And that's why you are after them?"

He nodded. "For the girls."

Ben found it hard to conceive of anyone reaching the depths of human behavior that the man described, but here it was in front of him.

"Where are the kids?"

"Split up. One of the boys was killed, but the rest went in different directions."

Ben felt sick. "What then?" It was hard to talk, but he managed to get it out.

"Some of us stayed here. The others went after a group of four."

"Where?"

"They went east across the desert."

"Did you see this group?"

"From a distance."

"Can you describe them?"

"Not really. Two guys, two girls. One of the guys was black and both of the girls had shiny black hair. That's all I can tell you."

Cat and Yuki! It had to be. And one of the boys was Wade. So the other had to be Simon.

"How long will your people follow until they turn back?"

"They won't turn back. They see what they want, they'll keep going until they get it. They have nothing to lose."

"Those kids are experienced in the wild."

"And those guys are excellent trackers. We spent a lot of years hunting in the hills around us. They can pick up any kind of track."

Ben was silent as he digested everything. It had been three weeks since the kids escaped.

"You don't get it," the man continued. "There are almost thirty guys following them and they've been gone a while. The boys are probably dead by now, and the girls ... well ..."

Ben jumped up and attacked the man with all the fury that a father could have. He began pounding on the man, punching him in the face, the neck, and the head. He didn't even feel Aaron and Sean pull him off the man.

The miner was doubled over in pain, his face a sheet of blood. He looked back at Ben through slits in his puffy eyes.

"Finish the job," he said, choking on his own blood. "Just kill me."

"I'd love to," said Ben with venom in his tone. "Nothing I'd like better. Not only for my daughter, but for Clete and

Morgan. What gave you the right to take their lives?" He walked to the edge of the clearing to calm down.

The man was silent, blood still streaming from his wounds. He rose unsteadily to his feet, picking up a fist-sized rock, and charged toward Ben, who was now across the clearing, thirty feet away. The man howled as he approached.

With one swift action, Aaron pulled out his pistol and put two bullets into the man, dropping him to the ground. Sean went to the man and felt his pulse.

"Dead. He got his wish."

"Is that why he attacked?" asked Ben.

"Of course. He knew we were going to kill him. He just wanted his miserable life over and he knew this would be the fastest way. You have to feel bad for him, but under the circumstances, I would have done the same thing."

"What do we do with the others?

Sean glanced at Aaron. "They killed two of our people," he said. "We can't take them with us. What would we do with prisoners? We can't let them go. If they ran across one of our kids, or just some unsuspecting traveler, who knows what they'd do to them? That would be on us. The problem is, we don't execute people."

"They're no longer people," said Ben, "and that guy said they were three of the worst of them, even before."

"Ah hell," said Aaron, pulling his gun out of its holster and turning in the direction the prisoners had been taken. "We know what we have to do. We have no choice."

Ben put his hand on his brother's arm. "No, let me. It's my job. Besides, I had to do this once before. I didn't feel guilt then and I won't now. It's just something that has to be done.

Besides, if he's right, we might have a lot more of them to deal with."

Aaron nodded his head and put his gun away, while Ben retreated into the darkness. A few minutes later, Aaron heard three single shots.

*****

The next morning, they gave Dan and Angus directions to the town in Yellowstone and let them know that the townspeople could provide them with information on the other communities across the country.

Ben and Lila embraced their old friend, knowing they probably would never see him again once he returned to Scotland. They watched as the caravan headed north, most of the people on horseback, with the line of silent electric tractors with their trailers full of solar equipment trailing behind.

Ben was subdued as his group pulled out and headed south to the spot where Harry had indicated the kids were attacked. Lila knew to leave Ben alone to deal with his demons. Once again, their peaceful life had been interrupted by violence. This time, it had been totally unexpected, since the world had known peace for so many years.

The next day they reached the area on Harry's map. They spent hours searching for the exact spot of the attack, and had almost given up when they heard a voice from the trees.

"Mom? Dad?"

Emma came running from the woods, followed immediately by Diana and John. They rushed into their parents' waiting arms. Tears and long hugs followed.

When the reunion was finished, Ben and Lila asked the teens to explain what happened. Diana described the attack and the death of Morgan.

"We hid deep in the woods and watched and waited for the men to leave. A big group of them went east, which is where we think Cat, Simon, Wade, and Yuki went. The rest of them hung around here. After a couple of days, they headed back north. We waited a whole day in the woods until we were sure they were gone. Then we came out and buried Morgan."

Emma began to cry.

"Emma and Morgan had gotten close," explained John. "This has been tough on her."

"What have you eaten?" asked one of the parents. "You all look emaciated."

"Mostly plants. We found some berries and have been living off them. We didn't want to shoot our guns or cook food on a fire—anything that could draw the men back. So we're pretty hungry."

Sean started a fire to cook some of the meat Dan and Angus had left with them. "You don't have to worry about them," he said. "They are gone."

"What about Zack and Darcy?" asked Zack's mother.

"We don't know. We saw Darcy riding away, and we think we saw Zack following her soon after, but we haven't seen them since. We thought we should stay here in case they showed up."

"And the others headed east?" asked Simon's father.

"As far as we know. I know the desert is that way, but I don't know if they crossed it. A lot of men went after them, and none have come back, so I don't know what it means."

The next morning, the three teens and their parents headed back north. They figured they could intercept the Scottish crowd and guide them into Yellowstone.

Zack's parents and a couple of the others headed south in the hopes of intercepting Zack and Darcy, while Ben, Lila, and the rest of the group traveled east and quickly picked up the trails of their children and the miners, leading them to the edge of the desert. The trail was old, but it was clear where they had gone.

"We're going across the desert," stated Ben. "Let's hope we can still catch them in time."

Chapter 25

Immediately after leaving his friends to go in pursuit of the fleeing Darcy, Zack found himself once again under fire. Bullets were flying around him, so he stayed low in the saddle. Suddenly, he felt a burning pain in his side. He'd been hit. He started to slide off the saddle, but hung on, the thought of Clete's torture occupying his mind. If he fell, that would be the end.

Somehow he kept going, holding tightly to his horse's mane. Darcy was out there somewhere and she was so young and probably the most helpless of the group. She would never survive on her own. The things she was good at—the skills she inherited from her mother—wouldn't do her any good if she was lost in the wilderness.

The shooting stopped. He was out of range. Well, he wasn't dead. He looked down at his side. He was bleeding profusely. He was going to have to stop soon and try to block the flow. But he also had to find Darcy.

The trip had been a disaster almost from the beginning. The worst part was that it was his idea. Because of him, Morgan was most likely dead—if he wasn't dead when he hit the ground, he would surely be dead by now at the hands of those men. And then there was the breakup of the group. They were all friends when they left—with the possible exception of Morgan—and now look at what happened. A rift between brothers; dissention, with John, Diana, and Emma not sure who to follow. Now Emma, who most likely had just had sex for the first time, saw her lover die before her eyes.

Only the foursome of Cat, Simon, Wade, and Yuki still seemed strong. He had underestimated them. They all had. They all knew that Cat had a special connection with animals, but she had always seemed ill at ease around humans. As it turned out, she was the strongest of them all, maybe with the exception of Simon—another person they all underestimated.

But it was all Zack's fault. The thought made him want to slip out of the saddle and die along the side of the trail. But he couldn't. He had to find Darcy. She was his responsibility.

He thought he heard his name. He slowed his horse and listened. There, he heard it again. He was dangerously close to passing out. His mind might be playing tricks on him. Finally, he saw her. Darcy rode out of the woods. She had been crying. For that matter, he probably had been too.

"Zack, you're bleeding."

That was the last thing he remembered before he passed out.

*****

It was dark when Zack came to his senses. His side was killing him. He was cold, despite a fire burning nearby. Where was he? He tried to raise up on his elbows, but it was too painful and he fell back down. He turned his head the best he could. He saw the fire, but between him and the fire was a pile of clothes. No, it was a person. It started to come back to him. It was Darcy. He could see the rise and fall of her body as she breathed. She was sound asleep.

Zack looked down at his side. There was a large bandage covering the wound. It was poorly applied, but it seemed to have done the job. He didn't appear to be bleeding.

He fell asleep. When he awoke, he could see the beginnings of dawn—maybe four or five o'clock?

"You're awake."

Zack saw Darcy kneeling next to him, tears running down her cheeks.

"I didn't know if you were going to live. You were really hot last night, and then you got really cold."

"Where are we?"

"As deep into the woods as I could bring you. I've been worried all night that those men would find us."

Zack thought back to the day before. The men wouldn't know how far they'd gone. They wouldn't have followed. At least he was pretty sure they wouldn't follow. Well, there wasn't much they could do about it right now. Not until he could travel.

"You stopped the blood," he said to Darcy.

"I think I did a shitty job with the bandage."

She had.

"You did fine."

Suddenly he was tired again and felt himself drifting off.

He awoke to bright sunlight. Darcy had her back to him and was holding her rifle and looking into the woods.

"Could I have some water?"

She looked back him with relief on her face. She set the rifle down next to Zack and got a canteen from one of the saddles sitting on the ground.

Zack was impressed. She had stripped the saddles off and tied the horses to a branch near some grass. Early in the trip, she had always convinced someone else to do that for her.

He said as much to her, finishing with, "You're more capable than I thought."

"I know what everyone thinks I'm capable of … the only thing I'm good at."

"I never said that."

"No, you didn't. Morgan did."

Images of Morgan, lying on the ground bleeding, made Zack want to start crying, but it was important that he remain strong.

"Is that why you two broke up? You never told me."

"You never asked. You were just interested in sex."

"Actually I wasn't. I just wanted companionship. I felt I had let everyone down with Morgan pretty much taking over. You made me feel like less of a loser."

Darcy stared at him. "No one has ever thought of me that way. Morgan didn't. He wanted me to … to do things. Weird things. When I refused, he said I was a whore, just like my mother. He was right. I just didn't want to hear it."

"You're not."

"I am. When I came to you, I wanted to have sex, not because I really wanted to, but because I didn't know what else to do. It was my one skill. Thanks, Mom. You did a great job raising me."

"Now you have more skills. You patched up my wound, built a fire, took the saddles off the horses, and guarded me."

Darcy gave a pleased smile. "Thank you."

"When you covered the wound, did you clean it?"

"As best I could with some soap. I had to do it carefully."

"Were there two holes or one?"

"Two. You must have two bullets inside you."

"No, I was only hit once. It means the bullet exited. That's a good thing. I don't have a bullet inside me."

He took in his surroundings and made a decision.

"Can you saddle the horses?"

"Of course. That's another skill."

"Good. Saddle up. We've got to leave here."

"But you shouldn't move."

"I have too. We need to put a lot more miles between us and those men. I don't think they followed us, but we need to get further away."

"Your wound will start bleeding."

"I have to take that chance."

"I can't lose you."

"You won't. I promise."

She gave him a doubtful look, but went about the process of saddling the horses. Zack slowly stood up. Leaning against a tree, he checked the bandage. Darcy really had done a crummy job. He had to smile though. He wasn't sure Darcy had ever done anything constructive in her life. It wasn't surprising, given her mother. In all honestly, he wasn't sure how the mother and daughter had even lived as long as they had. No, that wasn't true. Darcy's mother had the unique ability to get men to do things for her, as long as she reciprocated the only way she knew how.

He watched Darcy struggle with the saddle for his horse. She was trying so hard to be an adult. He was suddenly sorry that he had had sex with her. She was only fourteen and he had taken advantage of her. He felt ashamed.

He carefully peeled off the bandage. There was a lot of dried blood and the process of taking off the bandage started the wound bleeding again. He hobbled over to his horse and reached into his saddlebag for a clean bandage. He also found two strips of cloth to tie around the bandage to hold it in place. Darcy saw what he was about to do and came over to help. As she held the bandage in place, Zack tied the strips of cloth tightly around his body. Between the strips of cloth and the drying blood, he was sure the bandage would stay in place.

Darcy was finished saddling the horses. Zack checked the job she had done. He didn't want to be a mile down the trail, only to have the saddle slip off to the side and find himself face first in the dirt. But he needn't have worried. He made a few minor adjustments, but was impressed by the job she had done. He told her so. She was pleased to get the compliment, but put herself down in the process.

"I feel so helpless. You wouldn't have even had to check the saddle if Emma or Diana had done it—or Cat. Oh my God, Cat. She's only two years older than me, but she can do anything."

"Cat's not perfect either," said Zack. "Don't compare yourself. We've all had different backgrounds. Look at her parents and now look at your mother. You had no control over your situation any more than she did with her parents or I did with mine. We're on our own right now and you are stepping up. You'll make some mistakes, but you'll do fine. Don't be so hard on yourself."

Darcy couldn't help wondering what she had ever seen in Morgan. Zack was kind and supportive. Morgan was controlling. If she had to be in this situation, she was glad it was with Zack.

She helped him into the saddle. He cried out in pain as he swung his leg over the top, but once he was seated, he seemed to be okay.

"We'll go slowly," Darcy said. "I don't want you hurting yourself."

"Okay, doctor."

Darcy blushed.

Zack had to smile. With a little encouragement, Darcy was now asserting herself. Good. He had to encourage her to do it more.

"You're right. We'll take it easy."

"Which way?"

"Let's keep on going south. Eventually we can turn east."

"Not west?"

"I think we can abandon that idea. That was okay when there was a large group of us and we were exploring. Now we're just trying to survive. There are towns all over the country east of here, but we have no idea what's to the west."

"That makes sense."

They rode all day, stopping frequently for Zack to rest and check his bandages. As time went on, the bleeding dissipated, but it was still painful. Zack checked the map frequently.

"At some point we are going to have to cross some desert if we turn east."

Darcy was looking over his shoulder.

"The Grand Canyon," she said. "I've always heard the adults talk about the Grand Canyon and I read about it in school. I'd like to see it. Would that be okay?"

"You don't have to ask. You are one half of this duo. Your opinion is just as important as mine."

Zack was seeing a side of Darcy he hadn't seen before. He doubted anyone had ever seen it. She had grown up ashamed of her mother. Darcy herself had often been the butt of jokes. But now, given a little freedom and a lot of responsibility, she was thriving.

They ran across small towns from time to time—at least, what was left of the towns. In one they found a drugstore that was still standing. They searched it carefully, knowing that they couldn't trust the integrity of the building. Most of what remained in the store was worthless to them, but they found a few items of use, mostly in the first-aid section. There were many packages of gauze bandages. There was tape for the bandages, but Zack wasn't sure if it was still any good. He opened one package. After all those years, the adhesive had degraded and it was useless. There were elastic wraps, for ankle sprains and such. The elastic had long ago dried up, but the fabric could still be used to hold a bandage in place. They found numerous small items, including scissors, matches, and soap. The most useful item they found was water—cases of bottled water. They opened one bottle and tasted it. It was okay. It had a funny, slightly chemical taste. It was nothing like the fresh water they were used to, but it might save their lives if they hit a long stretch of desert with no water holes. They found some cloth bags and filled them with water bottles and the bandages, tucking some soap and a few of the other small things into their saddlebags.

They rode for many days, taking plenty of time to rest, eventually reaching the rim of the Grand Canyon.

"Oh my God," said Darcy. "This is amazing! It's like a whole different world."

They ran across an information center. Much of it was in shambles, but they were able to find a map of the Grand Canyon. Using the map, they explored the canyons, losing track of the days. At night, their campfire would flicker against the canyon walls, creating a beautiful, almost spooky atmosphere. They no longer worried that they were being pursued. Zack wasn't sure they ever had been, after that volley of gunfire when he'd been shot.

Zack's wound was healing nicely and each day he felt a little stronger than the day before. Something else was happening. He was falling in love with Darcy. Away from her stifling life in Yellowstone, she was coming alive. He was finding her a caring, sensitive woman—she had gone beyond the "girl" stage. In turn, Darcy was devoted to Zack.

"I don't want to go home," she said one night by the fire. "That's not even home to me. The thought of going back there scares me."

"It's because you're not the same person you once were. You've found the real you and you are afraid that you would lose that person if you went back."

Darcy nodded.

"Why should we go back?" Zack asked. "We've found each other. I've fallen in love with you."

Darcy's eyes lit up. She reached over and took his hand.

"I say we just keep traveling for a while," said Zack. "Our parents, and most of the others, did a lot of traveling after the event. There's nothing to say we can't do that. If we run across a town that's part of the Pony Express route, we can send our parents letters to let them know we are okay."

"Not my mother. I don't care about her. She never cared about me."

"Okay. Maybe at some point we'll find a town we want to live in. Until then, we just discover the country."

Darcy leaned over and kissed Zack.

"It doesn't matter where we go. I've already found all that I want."

Chapter 26

Cat and her friends stopped twice during the night to rest. When daybreak hit, they were still trudging through the sand and the dust. They rode the horses sporadically, but the animals seemed as tired as the humans and they didn't want to run the risk of the horses collapsing.

At mid-morning they found another rock formation to rest against, but it provided little relief from the heat and the blistering sun. Simon climbed to the top and peered back the way they had come, shading his eyes against the glare, but to no avail.

Cat watched him as he climbed the rock and couldn't help thinking back to the day they had first met, and how he looked with his skinny arms and sunken chest. It had taken a long time, but he was now a strong, muscular man, and she admired him for it—not for the fact that he was muscular, but for the effort involved. Simon had to work three times as hard as anyone else to get the results he now displayed. And through it all, he never complained. He had spent so many years sick in bed and not able to do even the normal things that others could, getting himself healthy was a quest. The only time he ever had to be concerned was in the winter. His lungs, having been weak for so long, were still susceptible to infection. He would catch bronchitis at least once every winter.

Cat always knew that because she was a little different, her parents were forever worried that she would never find someone to share her life with. Well, she thought, they didn't ever have to worry again. She had found the love of her life.

"Hey..." shouted Simon.

The rest of the sentence never came. The bullet hit an inch from his foot, and a few seconds later they all heard the boom of a rifle.

Simon slid off the rock and hit the ground running.

"Move. Move. Move!" he shouted.

Tired horses or not, they climbed into their saddles and took off at a gallop. A few more shots were fired, but the teens were out of range by then. They rode a few miles until they felt their horses begin to falter under them. They had put enough distance between them and their pursuers to give themselves and their horses a rest.

Cat felt sick. She was dizzy and her head felt strange.

"You okay?" asked Simon.

Cat fell to her knees and threw up.

"Sunstroke," said Wade, approaching with a pan of water he was using for the horses. He took off a bandanna he was wearing, soaked it in the water, and laid it across Cat's face. "I wish we had some shade," he said. "You need to rest."

"I can keep going," she said.

"No, you can't," said Simon, looking very worried. He glanced at Wade, who shook his head. "But unfortunately,"

Simon continued, "we have no choice. We can't stand out here in the middle of the desert. We have to find some shade." He looked ahead. "We should reach the hills by tomorrow and be in the mountains soon after. I'm sorry, Cat, you just have to keep going. Get on Scooby and I'll take his reins and walk him."

She protested, as much for her horse's sake as for hers, but in the end she lost the battle and was helped onto Scooby. She slumped down with her head next to Scooby's neck and tried to let the waves of nausea pass. The others walked ahead, leading the horses.

A couple of hours later, they found a large rock formation with an overhang, allowing people and horses much needed relief from the sun. Cat slept fitfully, alternating between nausea and chills, but by evening she was feeling marginally better.

"We can't stay here any longer," said Wade. "We don't know how much time they made and how close they might be."

"I don't understand why they are following us," said Yuki. "It doesn't make sense."

"Maybe that's the problem," said Simon. "If these are the same people who tortured and killed Clete, then it would be useless for us to try to make sense of it at all. No rational human being would do something like that. In their heads, they have a reason."

They resumed their trek, now easier going in the cool of the evening. They walked all night. Toward morning, when they should have been at their most tired, they found themselves moving a little quicker. The ground had become rougher and they had to skirt around boulders. They were reaching the hills. By daybreak, the whole landscape had changed.

"We made it," said Cat quietly. She had been sick all night, but hadn't complained.

"We did," agreed Simon, giving her a hug. "I'd love to make a stand right here and pick them off when they reached the edge of the desert, but that wouldn't work."

"No," said Cat. "There are enough of them so that they could spread out and circle us."

"I bet if we keep going, we'll find a watering hole," said Wade, "and a safe place to take shelter."

With that to look forward to, they continued on. Once the sun rose, it was hot again, but nothing like it had been on the desert floor. As Cat began to feel better, she kept an eye out for animals. They were totally out of food, and they were hungry. It became Cat's responsibility simply because she had the crossbow. They didn't want to shoot a gun and alert the men behind them to their location. She managed to kill four rabbits.

Late in the afternoon they came upon the perfect resting place for the night—a secluded watering hole. It had a large patch of grass for the horses. The spot was high in the hills, with a protected ledge that looked out over their back trail. With a lookout on the ledge, it would be hard for their pursuers to sneak up on them. It was actually the horses who led them to the spot. They could smell the water and had stepped up their pace to a fast trot.

That night they rested. Cat and Simon prepared the rabbits and they all dug in hungrily. After eating, they explored the area around the water hole. They were happy to find a second pool of water further in against a cliff face. It was smaller, but deeper than the first and they took turns bathing in it. Cat was elected to take the first bath and couldn't wait to strip off the clothes she had been wearing for days. The water was cool and wonderful. They had decided not to contaminate it with soap, but to just enjoy the sensation. She kept it short, knowing that the others were anxious to take their turns. She had barely gotten out when Wade jumped in. Cat let herself drip dry, enjoying the feel of the breeze on her wet skin. The friends were comfortable enough with each other not to mind being naked for the others to see.

At all times, one of them was on the ledge looking out over the hills and the desert beyond for signs of their pursuers. It was close to midnight when Yuki, who was on the ledge, called out to the others.

"I see lights. I think it's a campfire."

The others were beside her in seconds.

Yuki pointed and the others followed her finger. It was hard to see at first, and then one by one they caught the flicker.

"Wow, good eyes," said Cat. She turned to the others. "A couple of miles?"

"About that, maybe," said Wade. "Too close, in any event. As soon as it gets light, we have to move. Let's hope the fire isn't a decoy to fool us while they are creeping closer."

"I doubt it," said Cat. "They have to be as tired as we are and they'd have as hard a time seeing in the dark."

They packed up, ready for a quick departure at first light. They tried to sleep, but by then it was impossible. The minute dawn arrived, they were more than ready to leave.

As each hour passed, they were heading higher in altitude. After days of open desert, the constant breeze and the rock-shaded terrain came as a relief. They constantly turned in their saddles scouring the land behind them, but there was no sign of their pursuers.

It was mid-afternoon and they were in the mountains. Cat was leading the way when she came over a rise and stopped short. She held up her hand for the others to stop. In front of her was a crack in the earth like none she had ever seen. It was almost a mile wide. But unlike most crevasses caused by the earthquake, as this one certainly had been, the crevasse floor was visible—not only visible, but accessible. It didn't look to Cat to be more than a hundred yards to the bottom.

They had no choice but to descend into the crevasse. Everything to the left and to the right was blocked by fallen rock.

"What happened here?" asked Simon. "It looks like the mountains crumbled."

Which was exactly what it looked like. Great piles of rubble that had broken off the surrounding mountains had created mountains of their own. It would be impossible to traverse the piles of sharp and slippery rocks.

"I guess we go down and try to find our way up the other side," said Cat.

A ledge wide enough for the horses had been naturally cut into the cliff face. It extended downward to the floor of the crevasse. One by one they walked their horses down the trail. Enough dirt had covered the trail over the years to prevent the horses from slipping. Nevertheless, they took it slowly. A half hour later, all four had reached the bottom.

The found themselves in a box canyon, with steep cliffs on all four sides. The left and right sides were not viable options for finding a way up, as the tops of the cliffs had the high patches of broken stone. The only possibility for finding a way to the top and moving beyond the crevasse was the opposite side of the canyon from where they descended. They mounted their horses and started on the mile-long trek to the other side.

The canyon floor was strewn with boulders, but was otherwise a smooth surface, making for easy riding. They reached the other side in no time, but were immediately disheartened to find no easy access to the top. The canyon walls were steep, with no place for a person to climb to the top, much less a trail for the horses.

"I think we have to go back to the other side and head back up the trail," said Simon, "and try to find some other way around these mountains."

"Backtracking will be dangerous," said Wade. "We don't know how close they are behind us. But you're right, there's no other way out of here."

"I'm sorry," said Cat. "It was my idea to come down here."

"Hey, it seemed like a good idea at the time," said Yuki. "None of us had any better suggestions."

They started back and were about halfway across when they saw movement at the top of the canyon ahead.

"Oh no," said Cat. "We're too late."

Suddenly, a couple dozen men appeared at the top of the trail. All had beards, many of them gray, and they all wore tattered clothes. Many appeared to be barefoot. A fleeting question went through Cat's head as to how they could have crossed the desert without shoes, but the thought was short-lived. Many of the men took positions at the top of the canyon wall, guns pointing down at them, while others scurried down the trail.

There was no way out!

Chapter 27

Cat looked around in desperation. They couldn't fight them in the open. They had to find someplace to make a stand. To their right against the far cliff wall was a pile of rocks. Simon saw it too.

"Over there," he said. "It's our only chance."

They turned their horses and headed toward the rocks, each keeping low in the saddle to make a smaller target. But no shots came.

They reached the rocks in a minute and Cat hoped there would be a place to hide the horses as well. Scooby was her friend and an integral part of her family. If he was exposed, they would surely kill him to block off any chance of escape.

However, she needn't have worried. The rocks were piled high close to the cliff face, but there was a cramped space just long enough for all of the horses between the rocks and the wall and out of the line of fire. Growing against the wall was a clump of large bushes. They jumped off the horses, tied them to the bushes, and crouched down behind the rocks.

The pile of rocks was about twenty feet high and thirty feet long and filled with nooks and crannies for them to position themselves in. They climbed up the pile and peered over the top. From their position they were unseen even by the men on the ridge.

"Try to stay as hidden as possible," said Wade. "They could shoot into the wall behind us and get us with ricochets. How about I take the far left. Yuki can be about five feet down on my right, then Cat, then Simon take the far right."

"I'm good with that," said Simon.

Still no bullets came.

"We're in a bad spot," said Yuki. "They can wait us out. At some point we're going to run out of food and water."

Cat looked at Simon. They all knew Yuki was right. There was nothing to say.

"Why haven't they fired?" asked Simon. At that moment a single bullet hit the rocks near his head. He ducked out of sight.

"Simon, are you okay?" asked Cat.

"I'm fine. Just a few rock chips in my face."

A moment later, the boom of another rifle split the air and a bullet ricocheted off a rock near Wade. Then the rest of the guns started firing, with bullets flying all around the heads of Wade and Simon. They kept low, with their heads covered.

After five minutes, the shower of bullets stopped.

"Simon, this is weird," said Cat. "All of the shots were directed toward you and Wade. Not one shot came at Yuki and me."

Simon and Wade looked at each other from opposite ends of the rocks. Almost at the same time, the light of understanding was switched on.

"Because they want Wade and me dead," said Simon.

"I don't understand," said Cat.

"Look out there," said Wade. "Do you see any women?"

Cat glanced at Yuki, then back at Wade. "Are you saying they want us?"

Simon answered. "We've been trying to figure out why they've been following us. They wouldn't come all this way just to kill us. Look at them. I bet it's been a long time for them."

"Oh my God!" said Yuki. "Well if they get this far, I'll kill myself before I'll go with them."

"It's going to be dark in a couple of hours," said Cat. "If they rush us in the dark, we're done for." She cocked her Winchester. "Well, if they're not going to shoot at me, then I'm going to get a few of them."

She climbed higher on the rocks to where she was almost visible to those in front of them. Nobody fired at her. She aimed up to the top of the cliff and fired off five rounds before the men scattered. Four of the five rounds hit their marks and two of the victims fell forward and dropped to the bottom of the cliff.

"Wow, I'd always heard you were good," said Wade. "Did your dad teach you?"

"My mom. My dad is better with a crossbow."

She saw movement out of the corner of her eye. She turned, aimed, and fired all in one movement. The man had made the unfortunate decision to cross between two boulders. He only made it halfway before falling dead in the dirt.

Cat ducked down and looked at Yuki, who was staring at her wide-eyed.

"What?"

"You just killed them."

"Uh, yeah."

"It doesn't bother you?"

Cat cocked her head to the side with a questioning expression.

"Why would it bother me?"

"Because you killed them."

"They are trying to kill Wade and Simon, and kidnap you and me."

Simon, seeing Cat's lack of understanding at Yuki's question, took over.

"Yuki, if a bear was attacking you, would you kill it?"

"Of course, but…"

"These people are attacking us."

"I know, but they are people, not animals."

"Well, I'm not so sure of that, but even so, what you are saying is that it's not okay for an animal to kill you, but it's okay for a person to kill you?"

"Well no, but I guess I'm surprised that Cat isn't more bothered by it."

"Frankly, I think she'd be more upset to kill the bear. Yuki, it's all how you look at it. These people are intent on killing us. They've made their choice. You may have to kill some of them yourself. Don't let it bother you. If you do, you will hesitate and it will be too late."

Yuki nodded slowly. Simon knew she had never dealt with anything like this. If they survived, he was confident that Yuki would have a completely different understanding of the difference between life and death.

The shooting stopped. Simon and Wade had ducked down,

leaving the attackers with no targets. The attackers themselves, seeing the result of Cat's marksmanship, had also hunkered down. It was clear to the teens that the men intended to wait them out.

After fidgeting in silence for a while, Yuki finally asked, "So what are we going to do?"

Getting no response, she said, "I'm scared. I don't want to die, but I don't want to be taken by them."

"We're all scared, but we're not going to die," said Wade. "We'll come up with something."

Cat was looking at the horses, trying to figure out if they could make a break for it, when her attention was diverted to the bushes. They were moving. She could understand motion in the bushes that the horses were tied to, but these had nothing tied to them. The movement was slight, but it was enough to give her pause. There was no wind, and yet they were moving. She watched them for a few more minutes just to make sure she wasn't imagining it.

"What are you looking at," asked Simon. "You seem to be staring into space."

"Actually, I'm not." She slid down the rocks and moved the horses out of the way. The others were looking at her with puzzled expressions.

"There's no breeze," she explained, "but these bushes are moving. There's only one explanation."

She moved the branches aside to reveal a pile of rocks instead of the smooth cliff wall. She held her hand up to the rocks. Cool air was coming through the cracks!

She stepped back and looked at the bushes.

"These bushes aren't growing here wild. There are no

others growing down here. I think these were planted here to cover up something. And there's air coming through the rocks. Like the bushes, I think the rocks were placed here. I think there's a cave on the other side. Those guys can't see us from out there. Let's try to take these rocks out."

Simon and Wade slid down.

"I'll keep watch," said Yuki.

There was a renewed enthusiasm among the teens as the three started pulling out the rocks. Some were quite large and it took two of them to remove them. Within minutes they knew that Cat's theory was correct. There was open space behind the rocks. They worked faster. The space was taking shape. When they finished, they had cleared an entrance just large enough for the horses to make it through. Based on the placement of the rocks, they figured the whole cave opening was about six feet high and four feet wide.

"We still have a couple hours of daylight, so they won't attack us yet," said Simon. "One of us should check it out before we commit ourselves to it."

"Not that we have much choice," said Cat, "but I agree. I'll go."

No one objected, so she reached into her saddlebag for a flashlight and started in. She shone the light all around the entrance to make sure no snakes were lurking in the shadows, then continued on.

The chamber she had entered was small, only about twenty feet square. Other than rocks and small boulders strewn around, it was empty. A tall, narrow opening at the rear led to a second chamber. She passed through and found herself in a much larger room, at least fifty feet wide and a hundred feet long. At the far end was another opening, larger than the first, leading to another chamber beyond.

She shone the light all around the second chamber and discovered the remnants of an old fire pit. She approached it. It hadn't been used for a very long time. All around it were piles of food wrappers and hundreds of empty food cans. She picked one up. *SpaghettiOs*. Another said *Dinty Moore Beef Stew*. The labels were hard to read and many of the cans didn't have labels at all. Like the fire pit, they'd been there a long time. There was also a huge pile of discarded liquor bottles. Scattered around were various bits of furniture, including a chair, a small table, a mattress, and a pile of blankets. Dozens of books were piled next to the mattress. She pointed the light into a corner and almost dropped it. A skeleton lay propped up against the wall. A gun was still in his hand and the back of his skull was missing. It was obvious what had happened.

"How's it going in there?" It was Simon's voice.

"I'm coming out." They could check out the rest of the cave later, but there was no doubt that this was where they had to make their stand.

Cat joined her friends at the entrance.

"It goes pretty far in. I just checked out the first two chambers, but there is at least one more beyond that. Someone was living in the second chamber a long time ago. His skeleton is there and it looks like he killed himself. Here's what I suggest: we bring the horses in here and try to close up the hole we made in the entrance. It won't stop them for long, but they might not see it at night, and even if they do, they're not going to risk entering it in the pitch black and getting picked off. That will buy us some time. We can explore what's beyond the second chamber. If it's a dead end, then we make our fight here, take them one by one as they come into the cave."

She continued. "But I don't think we'll have to. I could feel the air blowing. There's another entrance somewhere back there."

"I'm convinced," said Wade. "Let's do it."

An hour earlier, their future looked bleak. Now there was hope, and the teens had a renewed spirit. They called Yuki in, and she brought the horses inside, leading them into the second chamber. They heard her give a gasp.

"She's found the skeleton," said Cat.

Wade and Simon chuckled, not at the thought of Yuki finding the skeleton, but of Cat's matter-of-fact interpretation.

The other three entered the second chamber and shone their lights on the piles of empty food containers and then on the skeleton.

"What do you think?" asked Wade.

"I think he was afraid to venture out. I think he stayed in the cave until depression got the best of him, then he killed himself," answered Simon.

"Do you think he was exploring the cave when the event hit?" asked Cat.

Simon shone his light around the roof and sides of the cave.

"I don't think so," answered Simon. "I don't think this is an old cave. Look up at the ceiling. It's not smooth like a normal cave. It's almost like two gigantic rocks came together to form the cave. Look at all the debris in here. It's relatively new. I think the earthquake formed it. Maybe the dead guy found it and moved in."

From the third chamber came a cry from Yuki. "Oh my God! You've got to see this."

Cat, Simon, and Wade rushed through the entrance to the next chamber, and then stopped short.

Sitting in the middle of an enormous cavern was a town.

Chapter 28

It was really a part of a town, one street about two blocks long. Most of the rest of the cavern consisted of rocks—rubble that had poured down from crumbling mountains. Under the rubble was the rest of the town, but the two-block section of a main street was remarkably clear of debris. Some of the buildings were partially caved in and rocks littered the street, but a few of the buildings were intact. Cat could tell by the style of the buildings and from what was left that it hadn't been a large town to begin with. The two-block section that survived seemed to be the center of town, but only consisted of a half dozen stores.

It was light in the cavern, and Cat looked up to see a space in the rock that allowed the sun to shine in. Less than a mile in the distance was an opening with light shining through it, telling them it led outside.

Nobody said anything at first, all of them trying to comprehend what they were seeing.

"How did it get in here?" Cat finally said.

Simon, who was also looking at the roof of the cavern,

came up with the explanation.

"I think the town was built in a small valley between two mountains. When the earthquake hit, the mountains shifted. I don't think this is a cave at all. I think the mountains fell in on themselves and created a roof at the center point. In the shifting, a lot of the rock fell away, crushing everything that was not in that center point."

"Do you think it will eventually collapse in the center as well?" asked Yuki.

"I would think so. Maybe not anytime soon, but yes, eventually. If another earthquake hits, it will probably collapse. If I had to guess, I'd say our skeleton friend in the cave came to the same conclusion, which is why he lived in the cave and not the town."

"Do you think he closed up the cave entrance and planted the bushes?"

"If I had to guess, he had no idea what had just happened. He was either from this town or came upon it. All he knew was that everyone he ran across was dead. It must have been a real shock."

"Like it was to our parents," said Cat.

"Exactly. The difference is, they eventually found other people in the same boat. Being out here in the middle of nowhere, this guy probably didn't even have anyone to talk to about it. He was probably scared out of his mind. Then after the earthquake hit and he found the cave, he was probably too scared to leave it, other than to get supplies from the town. He didn't know who was out there, so he planted the bushes, then blocked the entrance. After a while, he probably went crazy. That's when he killed himself."

"Or herself. We don't really know."

"That's true. I don't know the difference between a male and a female skeleton."

They walked the horses down a gentle slope to the valley floor (or cave floor—they weren't sure what to call it). They walked slowly down the main street, dodging boulders in the road and looking at the establishments. The first one they came to was a small grocery store. They shone their lights into the doorway and the window frames that were once glassed in. Many of the shelves were almost bare.

"This is where skeleton man found his food," said Wade.

"And this is where he found his booze," said Simon, shining his light into a liquor store across the road.

"Notice the skeletons?" asked Wade. "You don't see them very often." He looked at Simon. "Because it's a cave, or almost a cave, and it's cooler?"

Cat noticed that they were all looking to Simon for information on a more frequent basis. Because of having spent his early life indoors reading, he tended to be more knowledgeable on certain subjects.

"I think so. It's cool in here and it doesn't get any direct sun. I think the bones are preserved better."

There weren't, however, a lot of skeletons, further adding to the theory that the town was very small. There were two pickup trucks parked on the road. One had a boulder where the cab used to be, but the other was in reasonably good shape. It was rusted, but not as badly as most of the others they had run across.

In all, the town, like most they had seen, was eerie, and they weren't comfortable sticking around. They were anxious to leave, but Cat stopped them.

"We have a decision to make. We can continue on and leave this place, but if we do, we haven't helped our situation. Eventually the men out there will storm our little hiding place behind the rocks and find us gone. It won't take them long to discover the cave entrance. If we're gone, they will come through and continue chasing us. But we have the perfect opportunity to better our odds if we stay in the cave and wait for them. They can only come through the entrance a couple at a time. We wait at the beginning of the second chamber and pick them off as they come in. We can keep the horses down here. When we feel we've whittled down their numbers enough and they become too scared to enter the cave, we leave."

Simon was nodding.

"It's not perfect, but it will help our situation. We only need two of us. Why don't Cat and I stay in the cave and the two of you explore what's outside the opening at the end of the road?"

The plan agreed on, Cat and Simon left their horses tied to a post in front of one of the buildings and headed back up to the cave, while Wade and Yuki continued on.

"Will it work?" asked Cat as they climbed the slope.

"Your idea. You tell me."

Cat looked at him with a shocked expression.

"Just kidding. You really have to work on your sense of humor. I think it will. Once they know they can't get in without getting massacred, they will either turn around and go home, figuring we are not worth the trouble, or they will wait and wait and wait, not knowing what to do. Then we can slip out knowing we've killed some of them and the rest of them might take days to venture in again. As I said, not a perfect plan, but probably the best option we have at the moment."

They walked into the cave carefully, just in case the men had already entered, but it was dark and quiet. They entered the first chamber and listened through spaces in the rocks. Somebody was calling to them to come out from behind the rocks. They promised no one would be hurt.

"Right," said Simon. "Like we'd believe that."

"Are you thinking they'll attack at night?"

"I think so. It's the most logical time and I'd bet they don't want to wait out another day."

The sun was going down. They talked to keep the nervousness at bay.

"Do you think the others made it?" asked Cat.

"I hope so. If the men chasing us comprise the whole group, then there's a good chance they did. Even if some of that group were left behind, I'd like to think all of our friends got away. After all, like us, they were on horseback and these guys aren't."

"The trip sure didn't turn out the way we planned."

"No, but maybe it's good that we ran across this group. Maybe they would have attacked Yellowstone. If we can make a dent in their numbers, it has to be a good thing."

They could see through the cracks in the stones at the entrance that darkness had fallen.

"Soon, I would think," said Simon.

A few minutes later, they heard a commotion outside the entrance. Men were yelling and swearing, and they could hear rocks falling as they climbed the rock pile looking for Cat and her friends.

"What the fuck?"

"Where the hell did they go?"

They heard the bushes being moved.

"They're in here. There's a cave behind here."

"Tricky bastards. They piled up the rocks."

"They think we wouldn't notice? Pull down the rocks and let's go in."

"Yeah, and get ourselves shot up? You've got shit for brains."

"They're long gone. They wouldn't stick around."

"We don't know that. You saw how that black-haired girl shot. She was good."

"Yeah, I want to get me a piece of that."

"A bullet?"

"The girl, you asshole."

Suddenly there was quiet. Cat heard the men moving away.

"They're coming up with a plan," said Simon.

"We're ready."

They weren't.

It was the one thing they didn't plan for. They moved back to the second chamber, one on each side of the entrance to the chamber, and waited. After five minutes of silence, suddenly an explosion ripped through the rocks in the entrance, sending them flying in all directions. The noise was deafening, and smoke and dust filled the first two chambers. Cat was holding her ears and coughing. She looked for Simon, but couldn't see him through the dust.

The men were smarter than Cat had given them credit for.

They knew it was foolhardy to come in one or two at a time. She also never considered that they might have explosives. This way, they could charge in as a group.

As the dust began to clear, they heard movement in the front chamber. It suddenly occurred to Cat that the men had to be careful. If their purpose was to kill the men but not the women, they couldn't shoot randomly. Now she could see Simon. He nodded.

Cat aimed at the closest shape she could make out and fired. The man screamed. She heard Simon shoot, and it was followed by a grunt. She heard his target hit the floor. The cave had cleared a bit and she could see men more clearly. She fired one shot after another until her rifle was empty. She pulled out her pistol and continued the barrage. The men in the first chamber were all down, but there were others at the cave entrance firing steadily into the cave. It no longer seemed to matter who they were shooting at.

Cat looked over at Simon and mouthed the words, "I have to reload."

He mouthed back, "Me too."

The attackers sensed a pause in the action and knew what was happening. They chose that moment to storm the cave, hoping to get Cat and Simon before they had a chance to reload. Cat looked at Simon in panic.

Simon yelled, "We've gotta go."

They ducked down and started toward the cave exit. Bullets were flying around them as they ran. As the men were able to see better, they focused their aim on Simon, with obvious plans for Cat, if they could catch her.

How Simon avoided getting hit was a mystery to Cat, but

just as the attackers poured into the second chamber and capture or death were imminent, the popping of M-16s came from the rear of the chamber. Wade and Yuki stood, shielded by the sides of the exit, shooting rapid fire into the crowd of men. Behind them, Cat and Simon heard screams and moans. Wade and Yuki lifted their weapons so Cat and Simon could get past, then continued their barrage of bullets.

They stopped shooting. Cat and Simon reloaded and joined them as they surveyed the scene. The chamber was heavy with smoke and the smell of gunpowder. Some of the men were lying motionless, while others were writhing in pain crying. If there were any others alive, they had retreated back to the cave entrance.

"Time to go," said Wade.

They ran down the slope, nobody saying a word. They retrieved the horses and galloped down the road until they reached the end of the town. A bright moon could be seen shining through the crack in the cave ceiling. It was so bright, it illuminated the whole town. When they felt they were out of range, they dismounted and looked back at the cave.

"How did you end up back there?" asked Cat, still out of breath from the gun battle.

"We were on our way back," said Wade. "We saw something that would take your breath away and we wanted to share it with you. Besides, just in case you needed help, we wanted to be close by. When we heard the explosion, we knew things hadn't gone as planned, so we got there as fast as we could."

"Your timing couldn't have been better. I thought we were dead."

Cat looked over at Yuki, who was shaking uncontrollably. She walked over to her friend and hugged her. "Thank you. I know that was especially hard for you."

"It wasn't as hard as I thought it would be. The two of you—two of my best friends in the world—were going to die if I wasn't willing to kill. The decision turned out to be easy. But I'm feeling it now." She sat down in the dirt and began to cry. Wade sat with her and held her.

Simon came over to Cat and gave her a hug. The two of them kissed deeply. Suddenly, Cat found herself crying. She looked at Simon and saw tears running down his cheeks.

"Well, we're in good shape," said Wade, trying to lighten the moment.

It worked. The tears turned into a laughter of relief that they all had made it out alive.

Cat looked back at the cave and saw by the light of the moon three men standing at the entrance. The men lifted their arms in the air, turned and headed back into the cave.

"They are giving up," said Cat. "They're not going to follow any longer."

"You don't think it is a trick?" asked Yuki, now somewhat composed.

"No. It's like a wild animal accepting defeat. Instead of going belly-up like an animal would, they are walking away. I think we're done with them. Besides, there can't be many of them left."

"And we'll never know who they were," said Simon.

"I don't care who they were," said Wade. "They're gone. And now, we've got something to show you."

Chapter 29

The exit from the town and the earthquake-created cave was larger than Cat had originally thought from a distance. It was half the width of the road that ran through the town. They threaded their way carefully through a field of boulders and loose rock, finally coming out on the other side into the moonshine. It was so bright, it seemed almost like daylight.

They halted their horses and sat in awe at the panorama before them. In her life in Yellowstone, Cat had seen some beautiful sights, but she wasn't sure anything could top this. Spread out before them was a long wide green valley between the mountains. Roaming the valley were hundreds of buffalo, not yet settled down for the night. Some were enormous in size with thick horns, and others were smaller, without horns. Cat assumed the smaller ones were the females. Dodging in and out of the legs of many of the females were calves.

"Whoa," mouthed Simon.

"Incredible," said Cat.

"We couldn't experience this alone," said Yuki. "We had to come back and get you."

They rode down a long slope until they reached the valley

floor. They stopped their horses next to a large rock formation, dismounted, and climbed up onto the rock. They dozed, one person always staying awake, just in case they were still being pursued. But deep down, they all felt the men were done. They would head back to where they came from or find a new place to call their own. Either way, they were sure they had seen the last of them.

Cat woke up to a brilliant sun. Whereas a day earlier they were doing everything possible to avoid the sun, this sun was different, almost healing. The buffalo, most of whom had laid down for the night, were now back on their feet and grazing.

"I have to touch them," said Cat.

"Um, probably not a good idea," said Simon. "I think they can be pretty ornery. It might be dangerous."

"I'll be fine." She slipped off the rock and approached the herd. She walked quietly among them, talking to them as she walked and reaching out and touching them. The buffalo barely acknowledged her presence. A little one came up to Cat and nuzzled her. The mother cast a wary eye on the situation, but didn't interfere. Cat continued on into the sea of buffalo. She was in heaven. She felt so at home with them. Some of them towered over her with their enormous heads and chipped and well-used horns. A couple seemed annoyed by her presence, but most of them accepted her without a thought. Finally she turned back and made her way to the rock. Her friends were awestruck.

"Only you," said Simon.

"You too. I've seen how you interact with animals. I bet they would have accepted you, as well."

"Maybe. I'll try it some other time."

"What now?" asked Wade. "It's just us now. Our friends are on their own. There's no way we are crossing that desert again. I might also add that I'm starving."

Simon looked out at the buffalo, then back up at the entrance to the cave with the town inside. "I think we always assumed the four of us were eventually going to break apart from the rest of them. I think that's happened. I say we continue on and see where it leads us."

"I love it here," said Cat.

"I do too," added Simon.

"It's beautiful," said Wade. "I bet there are other spots worth exploring around here. Let's go on and find a place to camp tonight. Meanwhile, we can try to find some food."

"Only the crossbow," said Cat. "I don't want the rifles disturbing the buffalo."

"Okay, then you're in charge of dinner."

They mounted up and continued down the valley, skirting the buffalo. They rode for an hour, the whole time alongside the buffalo. The herd was enormous. Their original estimate of hundreds of buffalo was way off the mark. They realized the herd comprised thousands of head. Finally they reached an offshoot—a canyon that veered to the right. It was about a mile wide, and even more lush than the valley they were in. No words were spoken. They all seemed to know that it was the way they needed to go.

They rode another two hours at a walking pace. Few words were said. Cat, in particular, seemed to the others to be in a different world, often trotting off to look at something that interested her. Eventually they ran across a pond. It seemed like a good place to take a break. They took the saddles off the horses, who had been wearing them way too long. The horses rejoiced in the freedom and went off to eat some of the rich grass.

"Fish," said Yuki, looking in the pond. "A lot of them."

"There's lunch, and dinner too," said Wade. "You guys rest. Yuki and I will catch some."

Left alone, Simon said, "Let's walk."

They journeyed out into the middle of the canyon, hand in hand. When they were far out of listening distance from Wade and Yuki, Simon said, "You want to live here, don't you?"

Cat looked back at him with eyes sparkling. "Oh, Simon, I love it here. I know we have the perfect life in Yellowstone, but there's something about this place that's calling to me, and I don't know what it is."

"I do. Yellowstone, as beautiful as it is, has too many people. You can ride out and be among the animals, but with the town and the school and the people, frankly, it's too civilized for you."

"You do know me, don't you?"

"I do."

"But it's not fair of me to bring this up to you, because I love you even more and I want to be with you."

"And what makes you think I want to stay in Yellowstone?"

"You don't?"

"Cat, when we started this trip, I think we both knew that there was a possibility we would find someplace we wanted to live. We never really talked about it, but I think we both knew it. I spent my whole childhood wishing I could live in the nature I could see outside my window. Yes, I agree,

Yellowstone is beautiful, but there is nothing to hold me there. Our parents are there, but there is nothing stopping us from taking a journey up to visit them from time to time."

"Or them coming down," said Cat. "I know my parents sometimes miss the days when they were on the road. Are you saying this would be okay with you?"

"More than okay."

They kissed. Cat pulled back and looked Simon in the eyes. "I don't think I've ever been so happy."

As they walked back, Cat asked, "What about Wade and Yuki? Do you think they would want to stay or go back? I don't see them the same way I see other people. I could live near them."

"Me too. Let's wait for the right moment to talk to them."

That moment came the minute they returned to the camp.

"Let me guess," said Wade. "You were talking about how much you love it here and don't really want to go home."

"It's that obvious?" asked Simon.

"You could hold up a sign and it wouldn't be more obvious."

"What about you and Yuki?"

"I don't know. We haven't talked about it. We'll have to let you know. Meanwhile, Yuki has already caught a half dozen fish and I have a fire going. All I can think of is food at the moment."

Cat and Simon suddenly realized just how hungry they were. While Wade cooked the fish, Simon filled everybody's canteens and Cat searched the saddlebags for eating utensils.

They gorged on fish and when they finished, they laid back in the sun and napped, deciding not to go any further that day.

They deserved the rest.

Cat was in the middle of her afternoon nap when she woke up to the sound of screaming. It was a ways off and it wasn't human. It was a bird, and it was obviously in distress. She quietly got up, strapped on her holster, and grabbed her crossbow and quiver of arrows. No one else was awake. It was the first time they had slept without someone on guard. She slipped out of camp and climbed some rocks until she reached a plateau. The screaming was louder. The bird was hurting. She hurried across the rocks, turned a bend and stopped suddenly. She was face to face with a large hawk. The hawk went silent as it looked Cat over. Cat could instantly see what the problem was. The bird had somehow gotten one talon stuck between two rocks. It must have slipped as it landed.

She started talking quietly to the bird, letting it know that she was there to help. He was having none of it, however, and pecked at her every time she got close. After ten minutes of talking by Cat, the bird began to settle down.

Cat got closer, set her crossbow down, and reached for the hawk's trapped leg. The hawk tried to peck her. As he did, Cat's left hand shot out and grabbed him by the beak, holding it shut. She put her second hand on the bird's back to try to comfort it. Whether he sensed it or he had just grown weary of fighting, he let Cat reach down and free the trapped leg. The moment the leg was free, Cat sat back. The hawk immediately flew off. But then he circled and landed in a tree nearby, watching Cat. Cat waved to the hawk.

On her way back to camp, she saw a flash of metal. She ducked down. The flash came from close by. She crept closer, staying hidden behind the rocks. When she arrived near the spot of the flash, she carefully looked over the rock. Twenty feet away was a man hiding behind a rock and staring down into Cat's camp. The man was older, with a long gray beard. He was shabbily dressed and wore no shoes. It was one of the group who had pursued them across the desert.

Cat felt a shiver of fear shoot through her body. She had been wrong. They hadn't given up at all. Would this ever end? She looked around and saw nobody else. Maybe she had a chance to end this now.

She crept around the rock. The man's back was toward her and he hadn't felt her presence. When she was ten feet away, she spoke quietly to him.

"I have a crossbow aimed at your back. It would be an easy shot for anyone, but I happen to be very, very good."

The man stiffened. He laid his rifle down next to him, raised his hands, and turned.

He was the ugliest man Cat had ever seen, and the breeze was blowing his stench her way. His face was mottled with purple sores. He had no teeth and his gums had receded, giving him a wizened look.

"Are you going to shoot?" His voice was high-pitched and he was hard to understand with no teeth.

"I don't know what I'm going to do with you. I was hoping this was all over. How many of you are …"

From behind her came the now-familiar screech of the hawk she had rescued. Cat jumped to the side just as another man came at her with a large stick. Lying on her side, she pulled the trigger on the crossbow. The man was only five feet away. The arrow caught him in the right eye. He was dead before he hit the ground. She quickly looked back at the first man. He had picked up his rifle and was bringing it to his shoulder. In one fluid motion, Cat pulled out her pistol and shot. The man hadn't even had time to aim. The bullet caught him in the chest, and he dropped with a grunt.

She looked around quickly, not seeing anyone else. Suddenly, from the direction of the camp, she heard a half dozen shots. She clamored over the rocks to get a good look, loading her crossbow as she went. Looking down on the camp, she saw three more of the attackers on the ground. Her friends seemed to be okay. Then she spied one more of the men hiding behind a large rock. He was unseen to Simon and the others. She took aim and fired, the arrow hitting him in the upper back. He fell over on his side. The others heard the sound of the crossbow and looked up at Cat.

"There was one more," she said.

Her friends came into the rocks, searching for any others, but found no sign of anyone else. When they were all together, they asked Cat what had happened. She explained about hearing the hawk's cries and freeing it, then seeing the man behind the rocks and the hawk screeching again.

"I don't know if the hawk was intentionally saving me from the second man—I don't even know if they can think like that—or if he was screaming because the man was in his territory. Maybe it was just a coincidence that the hawk cried at that second. Whatever the answer, that hawk saved my life."

Altogether there were six dead men, and they knew they had once and for all seen the end of them. There was no sign of any others.

"What should we do with the bodies," asked Yuki, who, from Cat's perspective, had lost her innocence very quickly.

“Leave them,” said Wade. “The wolves, coyotes, and mountain lions will appreciate the food.”

“If they can get past the smell,” added Simon. "Maybe only the vultures will want them."

That decision made, they decided they no longer wanted to camp there for the night, and started on their way.

*****

It was well into the next day when they heard it. It was a sound none of them had ever heard before.

They had been making their way through one small canyon after another—each seemingly more beautiful than the last. Wildlife was abundant. Buffalo were still scattered around, but the teens also saw deer, mountain goats, otters, and marmots. The grass was a deep green and they were never at a loss for ponds, lakes, and streams.

They were traveling in silence when they heard it. It was music and it was echoing off the cliffs around them. It was at times squeaky and at other times bold, full, and even haunting. It was one of the most beautiful sounds Cat had ever heard.

They rounded a bend and found the source. Standing on a ledge in the brilliant sunshine was a man. In his arms was a large bag with pipes sticking out from it. The man seemed to be making the music by blowing air through a tube into the bag.

He saw the movement of the horses out of the corner of his eye and lowered the pipes. As the teens approached, he raised his hand, acknowledging them. And then he looked directly at Cat.

“Lila?”

Chapter 30

He was in his forties, well built, with gray flecks in his sandy-colored hair. He had a slightly receding hairline and a close-cropped beard. He wore jeans, a t-shirt, and sandals.

"I'm sorry," he said, setting down the bagpipe and jumping down from the ledge. "Obviously you can't be Lila, but you look too much like her not to be family. You are her daughter, right?"

Cat nodded. Who was this man and how did he know her mom?

"I saw you as a baby. I don't remember your name."

"Cat. Back then I was known as Katie."

"Right. Katie. I remember now. My name is Peter. I knew your mom for a short time."

The realization hit her. Peter. Her mom had told her about Peter visiting her when her dad was captured in Washington. She had also confided in her about being so lonely, not knowing if Ben was even alive, she had spent some nights with him—nights that had filled her with guilt for years. Despite Peter's—and later Ben's—reassurances that she had done nothing wrong, she saw it as a sign of weakness. But Lila had never blamed Peter for any of it. She had said that he was a kind man.

Somehow Cat imagined that Peter wouldn't look so old. But of course he was younger then. It was sixteen years ago. She tried to picture him sixteen years younger and realized that he had probably been a very attractive man. For that matter, he still was … for an old person.

"Yes, my mom told me about you." Cat had once told Simon the story, so she knew he was aware of what was happening. Wade and Yuki were clueless and just sat quietly.

"How is your mom?" He hesitated. "Did your dad ever return?"

"He did." She gave him a condensed version of the reason her dad had been gone. "My mom and dad are good. We're living in Yellowstone."

"I heard there was a large community there." Changing subjects, he said, "I'm glad your dad returned. Your mom was very much in love with him."

"She still is."

She could sense a sadness about Peter, but couldn't put a finger on it. She didn't think it had to do with her mom. It was something else. She introduced Simon, Wade and Yuki.

"I'm happy to meet you. I don't see too many people out here—none, really—so it is certainly a pleasure. I have a place only about a mile from here. I'd love to have visitors. You all look hot and tired. I have a running shower."

At the word "shower," they all perked up.

"It's always running. It's a small waterfall. It's cold, but very refreshing. I have soap and everything."

They followed Peter through the valley, walking their

horses. Cat was amazed that much of what they had traveled through since leaving the desert seemed to be a series of valleys, rather than one long one. She mentioned that to Peter.

"The earthquakes around the country shifted much of the land and I know that some of the valleys were the result of that. We're pretty out of the way up here, which is why you don't see the remains of many towns."

Cat told him about the town in the mountain.

"I haven't seen that one," said Peter, "but believe it or not, I've seen another one like that—not in as good shape as yours, though. There were towns built against some of the mountains and when the earthquake hit, the mountains came tumbling down. I've run across a number of towns that were destroyed by rockslides."

They rounded a bend and came upon a fence, Beyond the fence were a couple of acres of vegetables in full production. Cat also saw what looked like apple trees.

"My garden. I fenced it in to keep the animals out. And there are a lot of animals. Sometimes it's effective and sometimes not. I'm constantly repairing breaks in it. I eat well during the summer, but I also do a lot of canning so I am never without vegetables, even in the dead of winter."

His house was half cave/half house. He had taken a shallow cave about ten feet above the ground and added onto the front, bringing the house down to the valley floor. The add-on was his living room and kitchen, and the cave served as a loft bedroom. The house was comfortably fixed up with items that Peter had had found in area towns. An outhouse sat to the side of the house. The waterfall shower was around the corner, just private enough. Normally, privacy wouldn't be much of a concern to Cat, but as much as she liked Peter, the fact that he once slept with her mother made her just a little uncomfortable.

The teens took turns showering. Wade and Yuki showered together, but Cat and Simon purposely avoided it. They were quickly realizing that it wasn't going to be long before they gave in and had sex. Although they hadn't verbalized it, they both knew that when they did finally make love, it would be in a special place at a special time.

Peter offered the teens his living room floor for the night, but while they appreciated the offer, they chose to set up their tents outside. They did eagerly accept Peter's offer of dinner. He served a delicious venison stew with homemade cornbread, followed by coffee.

"How did you learn to make the cornbread?" asked Simon.

"Books. I've done well growing corn and I use it mostly for baking. The bread is a little heavy, but it's better than nothing. I also make a mean tortilla."

"And the coffee?" asked Wade.

"Ah, the coffee. You kids don't know what real coffee tastes like. I've collected cans of coffee over the years from supermarkets that I've raided. Even sealed in a can, the years have made it stale. Even I don't know the difference anymore. I'm used to it. But what I wouldn't give for a cup of Dunkin Donuts coffee."

He got blank looks from the kids.

"Never mind. I'm dating myself."

Wade and Yuki soon retired to their tent, thanking Peter for all of his hospitality. Cat and Simon stayed, sensing that Peter wanted to talk more. They knew it had to be hard to live completely alone so far from anywhere.

*****

"So your mom is good?"

"She is. She lost an eye years ago in an accident and wears an eyepatch. She says it was difficult for a while, but she's gotten used to it. Everyone says it makes her look mysterious."

"If anyone can overcome that, it would be Lila. Why did you leave your place by the lake?"

"Forest fire. My parents said they were considering leaving anyway so that I could be around other kids. They love it in Yellowstone."

"Do you?"

"Sort of, but Simon and I want to find someplace even more remote. We don't really like being around people."

"I hear you. Are you looking around here?"

"It is beautiful here."

"About twenty miles northeast of here is a series of valleys and gorges with a river running through the center of them. Check them out. You'll never find anything more spectacular."

"Animals?"

"More than you can imagine."

There was silence for a minute. Cat still sensed that Peter wanted to say something.

"My mom says you saved her life," Cat finally said.

"Ha, your mom was just fine. I didn't save her. She didn't need saving. She was lonely and lost. She thought your dad was dead. She would have come out of it on her own if I never showed up." He hesitated. "What Lila never knew was that she saved my life."

"How?" asked Simon. He had been quiet to that point, feeling that this was some kind of connection between Cat and Peter that needed to play out.

"How." Peter said it more as a statement. "It's a long story."

Here it was, thought Cat. This was what Peter needed to get out. He was just waiting for the right moment.

"I gave your mom the impression that I was just travelling the country, observing what life had become. That was a lie … a huge lie. I was running."

"From what?"

"Myself, mostly. In a sense, I'm still running. Living here is a penance of sorts. You see…" Tears came to his eyes. "I'm partly at fault for all of this happening."

"All of what?" asked Simon.

He spread out his arms. "Everything. The event that happened seventeen years ago. The bomb. The devastation. The billions of people dead." He held up his hand to prevent them from asking questions. "When I met your mom, I was close to committing suicide. So close. I was actually trying to find a quiet spot in nature to do it. When I met Lila, all that changed. Somehow, that week I spent with her filled me with hope. It couldn't erase all I'd done, but I could somehow learn to forgive myself."

He took a breath. Cat and Simon remained silent.

"I worked for the government at the secret facility that was developing the bomb—the civilization-ending bomb. I had majored in engineering in college. One of the best and the brightest, they said. They offered me lots of money and told me that I'd be doing essential work for the government to help safe-guard the security of the country. You have to understand—and it might be hard for you, growing up in this new world—but everyone was scared. Terrorism was rampant in almost every country, including our own. Something needed to be done about it."

He seemed to drift back in time, then brought himself out of it. "Of course, it wasn't supposed to do what it did. The bomb, I mean. It was supposed to be used for a specific target—a surgical strike, so to speak, but covering a larger area. The facility was top secret, even to most of the members of the government. The president knew, of course, as did his cronies. We didn't know at first exactly what the bomb was going to be used for, but word eventually got around and we all—people like me who had been recruited—realized that it was going to be a lot more powerful than we thought. We each had our own little piece of the job, so we were never given the big picture. Once the word started circulating about its magnitude, it made some people—mostly the military people involved—even more fanatic about building it. For others, like me, it came as a shock to the system. Hell, why should I have been shocked? We were building a bomb. We all knew it. Who cared if it was a big one or a small one? A bomb is a bomb. Can I get you more coffee?"

The question came out of the blue and Cat realized that the story was hard for him. He had to take a mental break. He had been holding it in for many years and finally had an outlet. It was almost too much for him.

Cat and Simon declined, but Peter got up and made himself a cup from the water that had been sitting on the cook stove in the kitchen. When he returned to the living room, he apologized.

"I'm sorry. I didn't realize it was going to be this emotional for me."

He took a sip and set his cup down. "A few of us started to do a little digging. We couldn't believe the rumors we were hearing. The bomb was designed to take out the power grid not just for a small part of a terrorist-run country, but for almost half the world—Russia, China, Japan, North and South Korea—countries that were our enemies, but also those that were our friends. I don't know why, even to this day. World domination, maybe? Anyway, the more we uncovered, the more we realized the president was far more dangerous than any terrorist group. We knew we had to get the word out. But we were young and naïve. It wasn't so easy to go to the media outlets—I just realized that these are phrases you've probably never used, or even heard in your life. What I'm trying to say is that we tried to spread the word, to warn people. It didn't work. They found out who we were and eliminated us, one by one. I was the last one left and I ran."

He took another sip of coffee. His hands were trembling.

"Everyone was after me—the government, paid assassins, and the police. The reason was never revealed, but they convinced the police that I was a terrorist myself. You don't know how many times I came within a whisker of being caught ... or killed. I went as far underground as possible." He laughed. "That's a term you don't know. It means hiding. In this case though, it has a double meaning. I was literally underground in a tunnel when the bomb exploded. In a cruel cosmic joke, I was saved and billions of others died. The guilt that emerged was overwhelming. I wandered for almost a year trying to come to terms with it, but I had reached the end of the line. I couldn't live with the guilt any longer. And then I met Lila. Her strength and her total dedication to her daughter—you—touched me in a way nothing else had. I knew I would never be free of the guilt, but I could somehow come to terms with it. When I left after a week, I knew I wanted to live."

He shook his head. "At the same time, I couldn't live around people, so here I am."

"My dad was with the president when he died," said Cat.

"Really? I hope he killed him."

"He was sent to kill him, but before he could, the earthquake hit and the building fell on the president. My dad says he watched him die."

"Good." He stood up. "You kids must be exhausted."

As Cat and Simon got up, Peter said, "Thank you. Katie—Cat—isn't it funny that your mother saved me the first time, and now here you are, the spitting image of you mother back then, here to listen to my confession. Thank you."

*****

Cat and her friends rode out the next morning, heading northeast. If it was as beautiful twenty miles away as Peter had indicated, it might be where they would settle. If so, would they see Peter again? Cat knew it didn't matter. An important connection had been made and a story that had never been told came out, and while it was important for Peter to get it out, Cat realized it was equally important for her to hear it to connect the dots in her family history. All these years her mother thought she had succumbed to a moment of weakness. In fact, she did what she had done so well so many times over since the event happened—she saved yet another life.

Chapter 31

It took Ben, Lila, and the others three days to cross the desert. They changed mounts often and had made sure they had enough water for both themselves and their horses. The tracks were easy to follow. In addition to those of Cat and her friends, there were the footprints of about thirty men. After seeing the feet of the men they killed, Ben had no questions as to how they could have done it barefoot. They probably didn't even feel the heat.

They were scared. Cat and the three others were capable of handling themselves, but against what odds? Thirty to four was just too overwhelming. Their best bet would have been to stay ahead of their pursuers, but were they able to? Anything could have happened. Ben wasn't prepared to lose Cat, and if something had happened to any of the kids, there would be a slaughter when he caught up to the group of miners.

"Stay positive," said Lila, riding beside him.

"There you go, reading my thoughts again."

"Not hard. It was written all over your face. I have great faith in all of them. There aren't four smarter and more capable kids around. They will find a way to survive. They probably already have. Remember, we're two or three weeks behind them."

They found their first clue as to the group's resourcefulness when they arrived at the box canyon. At the top of the ridge were the bodies of two dead miners. Animals had gotten to the men, leaving the bloated forms badly mutilated. Flies by the thousands swarmed around the two men.

"Serves 'em right," said Wade's father. "Especially for what they did to Clete. God, I hope the kids are alright. We never should have let them go."

"Do you really believe that?" asked Lila.

He lowered his head. "No, I guess not. We're all proud of our kids and we know they can take care of themselves. Hell, we weren't much older—if that—when this all happened, and they have more skills than we had. I'm just worried … as I know we all are." He squeezed his wife's hand, then said to the others, "Let's go."

There were two more swarms of flies at the bottom of the cliff. They held their collective breath that these two bodies were also miners. They were. They also had to hold their breath from the smell.

"These guys stunk when they were alive," said Ben. "Hard to imagine it could be any worse, but it is."

"Over here."

Nick and Jason had wandered from the group and were now near the cave entrance.

"Someone had dynamite," said Nick, as the others approached. "They blew the opening."

"Well, they were miners," said Sean. He stood up in his saddle and looked around. "This is the only way out of here, so we have to assume the kids used it. The entrance had to be large enough for the horses. So why did the miners blow it?"

"I know," said Aaron, who had dismounted and was inspecting the entrance. "These are all small rocks. I think they were here to hide the entrance to the cave. See the bushes? Not much left of them, but they are the only bushes around—hardly natural. And they are in a straight line. The kids probably found the cave and made a small pathway through the rocks."

"The miners could have done the same thing," Linnea reasoned. "Why would they blow it open?"

Sean answered it. "Tactically, it was their only choice. They knew if they went through the opening one by one, they would most likely be cut down. The kids would have been waiting for them. In fact, they probably did try to go through singly, with disastrous results. What worries me is that the kids wouldn't have been expecting something like dynamite. Cross your fingers."

Ben, Sean, and Aaron led the way on foot, guns at the ready. Lila had wanted to be part of the first group, but Ben convinced her, because they would be moving in the dark, and because of her only having one good eye, to follow. She reluctantly agreed.

Ben was still searching the first chamber, checking out the few bodies, when he heard Aaron exclaim from the second chamber, "Holy shit!"

They all rushed in to see what Aaron was looking at. Their flashlights revealed a couple of dozen bodies. All of them were miners.

"Holy shit is right," said Ben. "I guess that answers the

question of how capable our kids are."

"Here is where they were," said Yuki's mother in heavily accented English.

Scattered around the exit to the chamber were dozens of shell casings.

"Think they got them all?" asked Jason.

"If not," answered Lila, "the miners would have been stupid to continue on. I can't imagine that there could have been more than a half dozen of them left."

"But they didn't turn back," said Sean. "We would have seen them. Assuming there were any left, this would now be a grudge match. They would have nothing to lose. I suggest we tread lightly and be aware. The last thing we need is to get caught in an ambush."

"Worse than that," said Mike jokingly, "our kids might have to save us."

The levity was appreciated, but they still left the cave and went into the half-buried town on high alert. While the town would normally have been of interest to them, they were too anxious to catch up to the teens to give it more than cursory attention.

When they ran across the bodies of the remaining miners in the rocks the next day, they were pretty sure the kids had ended it there, and they all began to breathe a little easier.

"I'm beginning to think they didn't need us after all," said Aaron.

"You think?" answered Ben.

With the terrain now easy to navigate and switching between horses, they were able to make good time. Late that day, they were rounding a bend and came across a lone man sitting on a rock. It only took them a second to determine that he wasn't one of the miners. They rode up to him slowly.

He looked them over and his face broke into a smile.

He pointed down the canyon.

"They went thataway."

*****

"Oh … my … God!" said Lila.

She dismounted and walked over to Peter, who had hopped off the rock.

"Howdy stranger," he said.

They hugged and Lila called Ben over and introduced the two men.

"Thank you," said Ben, shaking Peter's hand. "You kept her going so many years ago."

"I didn't, but that's a story for another time. Cat can tell you about it when you see her."

Ben and Lila both looked puzzled.

"It's a story I've only ever told once, and Cat and Simon were the only two to ever hear it. Thanks to them for taking the time to listen, I don't ever have to tell it again."

"Are Wade and Yuki with them?" asked Wade's mother nervously.

"They are, and all four are in good shape"

"Where are they?"

"If I had to guess, I'd say they are about twenty miles northeast of here. It's too late in the day for you to catch up to them, so I suggest you come and pitch your tents at my place and start fresh in the morning. I've just made a large batch of venison stew—your kids ate most of my last batch.

*****

They rode into the valley about noon. The first thing they saw was the river. It came out of the opposite side and then turned and meandered its way out of sight down the middle of the valley. The second thing they saw were the animals. A small herd of buffalo peacefully chewed some of the ankle-high rich green grass that covered the valley floor. In the distance dozens of deer drank from the water's edge. On the side of the river where they stood, a forest ran the length of the river as far as the eye could see. It ran up to the side of the valley wall a mile or two back from the flowing water.

On the other side of the river was the prairie, extending about the same distance to the rock walls on the other side. In the distance, along the wall under a large overhang, they could see two small specks. Tents!

They crossed the river in a shallow area and rode toward the tents. Now they could see horses with their heads down munching grass. And then they saw it—movement on top of the overhang. It was the kids, all four of them, and they were jumping up and down and waving.

Ben looked over at Lila as they rode just a little faster. "I never doubted she would be okay. After all, like mother, like daughter."

Chapter 32

It was two months later. Ben and Lila rode down the dusty road that led into the town of Paradise. Behind them, riding the two tractors with the trailers carrying the solar panels and generators, were Aaron and Sean, their horses tied behind the trailers.

Ben felt some nervousness, knowing that his presence, at least initially, would be met with various degrees of hate. It had been eight years since he had last set foot in Paradise, but he knew that to the residents time meant nothing when it came to a certain man named Ben.

They had observed the town from the hills outside town. The power plant was still there, a silent, blackened hulk. The area around the plant was devoid of activity. The focus of the town had shifted away from the empty building. The rest of the town looked remarkably clean and almost cheery. Flowers hung from porches and the town had a fresh feel to it. The word was that the town had been righted, purging itself of the negative elements. The population had swelled to almost 200, many of the additional numbers being children born over the last eight years. It paled in comparison to the high of over 500 when the town had power. But it was an unhappy 500—at times a violent 500.

Maybe he was wrong. Maybe they wouldn't hate him. After all, he was coming bearing gifts. But hate was a strong emotion, one that didn't always dissipate easily over time.

A crowd had formed in front of them, their attention as much on the tractors as the people.

"Hey Sean. Hey Aaron." An older man stepped out in front of them. Ben was ignored, even though he was in front.

"Hey Ozzie," said Aaron. "Got something for you."

"Don't want it."

"You don't know what it is."

"Don't matter. Don't want him," he said, pointing at Ben.

"Fine. There are other towns that might want it. Your loss."

Aaron turned his tractor around, Sean following suit.

Ben watched Ozzie. The old man was obviously torn, but his hatred had won out.

Ben turned his horse to follow the others when someone from the crowd called out, "Ozzie doesn't speak for all of us."

"Shut up. You're new. You don't know what this one did."

"Oh God, Ozzie, I've heard the story a million times, mostly from you. When are you going to let go of it?"

Ben broke in. "Look, I did what I did. Frankly, given the same circumstances, I'd do it again. Your community was a cancer on the landscape. People died because the people in charge of this town caused it to happen because of their greed. If I hadn't done what I did, who knows where you would be now? All the reports I get are that the town has become something special. The people here care about each other. We were given a gift recently and we wanted to share it with you, as a way to help with your resurgence. These are very powerful solar generators. The tractors are solar-powered as well. With the generators are very simple instructions on how to build more of them and how to build windmills. It'll take some work, but it can be done. A couple of years from now, this town could be totally electric again. The best thing is that you will all be in charge of it. You don't have to rely on anyone else telling you what you can and can't do."

He looked around the crowd, which now consisted of just about the whole town.

"So, as Aaron said, you can accept our gift in the spirit in which it is being given and get over your anger, or we will be happy to move on to another town and present them with it. Let's put an end to this, shall we?"

"As I said, Ozzie doesn't speak for the rest of us." The man turned to those around him and gauged their mood. "I think I can speak for everyone else when I say thank you. We very much appreciate the gifts. I hope the four of you will join me for dinner. I'm sure between us, we can put you up for the night."

"We will take you up on the dinner invitation," said Sean, "but we'll set up camp across the river. However, we'll be back in the morning to give you some training on the generators and help you make sense of the directions for building more. They are actually quite easy."

*****

Two days later, they were heading home and Ben was deep in thought.

"Your conscience is finally clear," said Aaron.

"It is. You know, over the years I've had to kill a lot of people and it bothered me less than blowing up their power plant. Maybe it's because it affected innocent people. It wasn't right. They didn't deserve it. It's troubled me for a long time."

"And now you've made it right."

"I have."

He looked around him at the sky, the landscape, and most of all, at Lila.

"Everything is right."

Epilogue

Lila and I go often to visit Cat and Simon in their new home in the valley. Wade and Yuki live just a mile away from them. Some of us journeyed down to help them build their houses. Like Peter, they were able to combine rock and wood, using rock overhangs as the rear rooms of their houses, and constructing wooden fronts.

They spent the fall preparing their gardens for the next spring, experiencing bumper crops their first year. Although we haven't seen him in our trips down, Cat says Peter comes by on occasion to visit. The kids have developed a nice relationship with him.

Cat told us Peter's story. That would be a hard one for him to get over, and in all honesty, I doubt he's over it. After all, knowing that you are partly responsible for the downfall of mankind is not exactly something you recover from. I think visiting Cat and the others is good therapy for him. I wish him luck.

Cat and Simon are married now. Lila performed the ceremony. It was actually a double ceremony as Wade and Yuki tied the knot as well. So far, no hint of kids. In fact, none of them seem much interested in having children. Some of the parents think that as they get older that will change, but Lila and I aren't so sure. They seem perfectly content to just be with each other and the animals. But then, the animals have always been Cat's first love.

In Yellowstone, things are good. People seem genuinely happy that we turned down most of the solar panels and the generators and kept only one for the doctor's office. Those are really more suited to areas not as spread out as Yellowstone, like Paradise or Monett—although we heard from Brian in Monett that they turned them down as well. They always seemed happy to forgo modern conveniences, so I wasn't surprised to learn that.

The Pony Express is working better than anyone ever expected. As far as we have determined, all of the communities in the United States have been accounted for. There are forty-six of them. Many are small, just a couple of dozen residents, but all are thriving. In fact, it was the small communities that were most excited about the solar and wind power, and that makes sense to me. When the larger communities got them working, they shared them with the smaller ones. I still have trouble believing the amount of cooperation I'm seeing all over the country—all over the world, if Angus and his crew are any indication. I have to wonder how long the cooperation will last. Luckily, the world population is so small, it will probably take several hundred years, at least, for the negative elements to rear their ugly heads again.

William and Harry both survived and are doing well. Emma, John, and Diana resumed their lives in Yellowstone and don't seem to have any desire to travel. We wondered for the longest time about Zack and Darcy. We assumed that they were still alive someplace, but they never returned home, much to the sadness of Zack's parents. Darcy's mother died—she had been ill for some time and died during a particularly cold spell during the winter—but she never seemed all that bothered by her daughter's disappearance. About a year after the fight with the miners, the Pony Express delivered a letter from Zack to his parents. The letter was sent from Monett, but he made it clear that they were just passing through, with no destination in mind. He spent the letter raving about Darcy, her growth, and their love for each other. When I told Cat about the letter, she said she wasn't surprised about Darcy. She said she always felt that Darcy had more inside her than most could see.

Cat told us the story of the trip and the conflict between Zack and Morgan. In their own ways, Zack and Darcy were in the process of becoming outcasts—if only in their own minds—and were probably perfect for each other. Who knows? Maybe they will show up one day.

The word from Paradise is that they have set up many windmills and have solar panels spread throughout the town. Morale is high and history has been forgotten, thank God! Knowing that they are doing well has eased a lot of the guilt I've felt over the years. Maybe someday it will be gone forever.

When I think of Cat and Simon and Wade and Yuki settling on their own pieces of heaven, I can't help thinking that after all this time, the planet has finally healed itself. It doesn't remember when we were trying to kill it. It has given us the chance to start over. The conflicts are gone; people genuinely want to help other people; and the young people who are growing up in this new world are stronger and more aware than we ever were.

I really can't predict the future, but based on what I can see around me now, I certainly have grounds for hope.

And I'll take it.

The End

ABOUT THE AUTHOR

Andrew Cunningham is the author of the Amazon bestselling thriller **Wisdom Spring** and the thrillers **All Lies** and **Deadly Shore**, as well as the post-apocalyptic *Eden Rising Trilogy*: **Eden Rising**, **Eden Lost**, and **Eden's Legacy**. As A.R. Cunningham, he has written the *Arthur MacArthur* series of mysteries for children. Born in England, Andrew was a long-time resident of Cape Cod. He now lives with his wife, Charlotte, in Florida. Please visit his website at *arcnovels.com*, and his Facebook page at *Author Andrew Cunningham*.

Made in the USA
Coppell, TX
15 April 2022

76586250R00154